SHELTER FOR BLYTHE

BADGE OF HONOR, BOOK 11

SUSAN STOKER

CHAPTER ONE

"*That* her?"

Sawyer "Squirrel" McClay turned to look at his friend and fellow firefighter, Penelope. She was sitting on one of the couches in the fire station with her pet miniature donkey, Smokey, beside her. The creature had found her when she was in the middle of nowhere, searching for their friend Erin and the asshole who had kidnapped her. Smokey had been smoldering from the forest fire raging around them. Penelope had poured water on the suffering animal and apparently that was all it took for Smokey to decide she was now *his* human.

Squirrel couldn't complain about the small donkey being around because he was obviously doing Penelope a lot of good. She was less jumpy, less likely to lose her temper with him and the others, and more relaxed.

Yup, it was unconventional to have a PTSD donkey, but what did he know?

Squirrel didn't hear any censure in Penelope's tone when she asked her question, so he nodded. "Yeah." He'd been texting Blythe nonstop for the last twenty minutes or so. Sometimes she liked to talk, but most of the time she preferred to communicate with him via text.

"You have any luck getting her off the streets?"

Squirrel pressed his lips together and shook his head. "No. And it kills me. I hate that she's out there by herself. Sleeping on the ground. Always having to watch her back."

"You talked to Quint about her, right? He have any luck in finding her?"

"No."

"Beth could track her through the cell phone, you know. All you have to do is ask."

Squirrel knew that. Hell, Beth had volunteered the second she'd heard about Blythe's situation. He'd taken her up on her offer, but was keeping that information to himself for now. He knew without a doubt that if Blythe found out he'd interfered in any way with her life, he'd never hear from her again. And that thought hurt. He'd gotten to know the woman pretty well over the last few months, and he wanted to believe that she wouldn't just disappear on him after all this time, but he couldn't take the chance.

She was special. More than special. And it literally hurt his heart when he thought about her being cold, hot, hungry, dirty, and in danger. And he knew from talking with both Tadd and Louise that living on the streets was definitely dangerous. The older couple had taken Blythe under their wing when they were living in an abandoned building next to a hospital.

The night Doctor Shane Kingsley had set fire to the building—the night Squirrel first met Blythe— had been more than chaotic. Tadd and Louise had ended up in the hospital and Blythe had disappeared in the confusion.

Squirrel had inadvertently given her his cell phone; it had been in the pocket of the sweatshirt he'd changed out of in the back of the fire truck on the way to the fire. With no thought other than getting her warm, he'd given Blythe his sweatshirt that night. He'd been annoyed at first when she'd disappeared with his phone, but decided the vulnerable woman needed it way more than he did.

So instead of calling his provider to cancel the phone and number, he simply got another cell. And then he began to text his old number, knowing texts would show up on the home screen, and she could see them without having to unlock the phone.

It had taken two weeks of constant texts before she'd finally replied. He'd given her the code to unlock his phone so she would have complete access. Yeah, she could still read his emails, and she'd been able to read texts from people before they'd received his new number, but he had nothing to hide.

The first time Blythe had responded, Squirrel had felt inordinately pleased. Her text had been short and to the point, but it was a start. She'd merely written, *You're insane.*

She'd only met him once, and even that encounter had been short. Squirrel knew giving her the phone and continuing to communicate with her was a bit odd, but it was refreshing to talk to someone who didn't want anything from him other than a simple conversation.

It seemed as if his entire life, he was the guy women wanted to be "friends" with. They wanted help with their homework. They wanted him to help set them up with his firefighter friends.

He wasn't an idiot. He knew what women saw when they looked at him. A tall, skinny guy with glasses. They judged him based on his looks alone without bothering to get to know him. He didn't fit what they thought they wanted...namely a gorgeous, tall, buff hunk of a man who would fall at their feet and worship them until they were old and gray.

The irony was that Squirrel knew when he found someone to love, he'd most certainly bend over backward to make sure they wanted for nothing. However, he wasn't the kind of man women normally looked at twice, so most often he never had a chance to show them he was more than the nerd they saw on the outside. When he went out with his firefighter buddies, all eyes were on them, not him.

It didn't bother Squirrel...usually.

But Blythe wasn't like that. Granted, she'd only seen him once, and it was in the middle of an intense situation, but she never asked him for anything, like the girls and women in college and high school had. Nothing other than his time to talk to her.

And that was what really got to him. For the first time ever, he *wanted* a woman to ask something of him, and Blythe steadfastly refused. He wanted to help her. Wanted to be the man she trusted to open up to about her hopes and dreams...and fears.

Squirrel knew Blythe was different than the women who wanted to use him for his knowledge or connections because she always sounded happy to talk to him when he called, always steering the conversation away from her situation. They'd had countless text conversations, and not once had she made him believe she was talking to him for any other reason than it pleased her.

He'd taken a screenshot of something she'd told him in a text once, pulling it up when he felt down or insecure.

Thanks for being my friend.

The thought of Blythe being his friend, and *only* his friend, was enough to make Squirrel's palms break out into a sweat. He'd never felt for a woman what he felt for Blythe. Maybe it was the late-night text conversations. Maybe it was that he'd gotten to know her as a person before even remotely thinking about having sex with her.

Whatever it was, Squirrel wanted her. Wanted to scoop her off the streets and tell her that he'd always keep her safe. That he'd make sure she had whatever she needed so she didn't have to sleep on the dirty ground anymore. It was similar to the feeling he remembered having when he saw his baby sister Emma for the first time, yet very different.

He didn't feel brotherly toward Blythe Coopman. Not in the least.

Penelope cleared her throat and when Squirrel looked up, he saw her eyebrows raised in question.

"Sorry, what?" he asked.

She smirked. "Beth could find her for you," she repeated.

Squirrel sighed. "I know. She already brought it up."

"And?" Penelope asked.

Running a hand through his short dark brown hair in agitation, Squirrel tried to put his feelings into words. "It would be a breach of trust. I've only talked to Blythe about her being homeless once. She told me in no uncertain terms that she was doing her best, and that she'd gotten herself into the situation and wanted to get herself out of it."

"But that's silly," Penelope said, her facial expression making it clear she didn't understand. "I mean, if you're willing to help her, why wouldn't she take it?"

"I haven't been in her shoes, but I'm thinking she doesn't want to be pitied. And taking money or other kinds of help would make her feel indebted to me. And she flat-out told me she doesn't ever want to be in debt to anyone else."

"Why? What happened?"

"I don't know. She wouldn't say. But obviously something that had a profound effect on her. I don't like it. Hell, I *hate* it. Every time I hang up with her or end a text conversation, I'm terrified it'll be the last time I talk to her. Anything could happen to her on the streets. She could be beaten up, raped, killed…but she always reassures me that she's being smart and safe." Squirrel sighed and looked at Penelope. "But I have a plan."

"A plan?" Penelope asked.

"Yup. I promised I wouldn't offer her money to get her off the street, but I never said I'd give up trying to keep her safe and get her back on her feet."

Penelope held up a hand, stopping Squirrel from saying anything else. "If you go behind her back and somehow trick her, and she finds out about it, you'll lose your chance with her forever."

"It's not like that," Squirrel protested, shocked at the absolute certainty in Penelope's voice.

"If you're going to be sneaky and somehow give her money, but don't tell her it's from you…it *is* like that. I don't know her, but it's obvious she's a proud woman. She's already told you that she doesn't want your money. If you think doing something under-handed is going to get her to like you, you're absolutely wrong."

Squirrel tried not to get upset at his friend. But she totally had the wrong idea. "Is it so wrong to want to help her?" he asked. "Wrong to want to make her life easier? I don't know what happened to put her on the streets, but it's obvious to everyone who's met her that she doesn't belong there."

"So others *do* belong there?" Penelope asked.

Exasperated, Squirrel shook his head. "No, that's not what I meant."

"Then say what you mean," she insisted, absently petting Smokey's head as she sat back on the cushions. As if the donkey could feel her agitation, he nuzzled closer, laying his head in her lap.

Squirrel wanted to laugh at the way the donkey was acting like a lapdog, but he was too upset. "It kills me that she'd rather sleep on the streets than accept my help. She means something to me. I've never felt about a woman the way I do about her. I want to get to know her better. Take her to dinner. Date. But knowing she doesn't feel the same way about me...it tears me up inside. I'm not trying to trick her. But even if she doesn't want my help, I'm going to do whatever I can to give it to her anyway."

Penelope stared at him for a long moment. Squirrel sat still and let her silently analyze him. He hadn't meant to blurt that out, but he wasn't sorry he had. He liked Blythe, and not simply because of her looks. Hell, she'd been dirty and disheveled the one time they'd met. It was *her*. Her quirky sense of humor. The way she put everyone else before herself. Her compassion and stubbornness.

Every time he had a conversation with her, Squirrel felt more and more desperate to get her off the streets.

"What's your plan?" Penelope asked softly, all traces of animosity in her tone gone.

"Tadd and Louise have moved out of Sophie's house. They got an apartment not too far from there. I asked Sophie, and she said she had no problem with Blythe moving in. She said she'd do whatever I needed her to do to help convince Blythe to accept. She'd be safe there, Tiger," Squirrel said, referring to the unoccupied home of their coworker's girlfriend. "She wouldn't have to worry about someone stealing her stuff. She wouldn't have to worry about someone attacking her in the middle of the night or raping her. Sophie and Chief live next door; if she needed anything, they'd be there to help her. I have no idea if she'll accept my offer, but I desperately want her to, even if she doesn't want anything to do with me personally. At least she'll be off the streets and safe."

He waited, holding his breath to see what Penelope thought.

"Actually...that's a good idea. Really good. Tadd and Louise took Sophie up on her offer for them to live there, and she seemed to be close to them. It's not really charity since Sophie isn't living there anyway."

Squirrel let out the breath he was holding. "Now I just have to figure out how to bring it up in conversation, and how to get her to agree."

"If you knew where she was, you could accidentally run into her. Or have Sophie do it."

Squirrel shook his head. "No, *that* would be underhanded and sneaky. I just have to man-up and bring it up in conversation."

"I do have a piece of advice for you," Penelope told him.

"What?"

"If you really like this woman, don't let her slip through your fingers. Life is short. You never know when you'll be minding your own business one second, and fighting for your life the next."

Squirrel immediately wanted to get up, step over the coffee table, and take the slight firefighter into his arms, but he knew she wouldn't appreciate it.

Penelope had come a long way since she'd been taken hostage by terrorists over in Turkey while in the Army. He wouldn't do or say anything that would make her believe he thought less of her and the way she'd handled everything.

"I'm not exactly a woman's ideal man. I might be a

firefighter, and I know some women like to fantasize about a man in uniform showing up at their house and telling them they've come to 'put out their fire.' But if it was *me* who showed up, they'd be disappointed."

"What? Why would you say that?" Penelope demanded.

Squirrel didn't beat around the bush. He knew what he was and what he wasn't. "Look at me, Tiger. I'm shorter than everyone else who works around here—and you don't count. I'm skinnier, not as muscular. And I wear glasses. I've seen the covers of those romance books you like to read. Not one of those hunks is wearing glasses."

"Squirrel, those aren't real. They're meant to sell books. They're just fantasies."

He arched his brows at her. "Yeah, that's what I'm saying. I'm no woman's fantasy."

"Oh...but—"

He cut her off before she could say anything else. "I'm not saying I don't think I have a lot to offer a woman. I do. I have a steady job that I'm good at. I have a great family. I own my house, even if it's not a mansion, and I would always put a woman first if she were in my life. I know women bitch about the media and the image of 'beauty' it portrays. Skinny, face full of makeup, high heels. But what about men? It's the same thing. I don't live up to—and will never live up to—the media's idea of the alpha male. I'm as alpha as Sledge, Crash, Chief, or even Moose, but because I don't look the part, most women won't even consider me as a mate."

Penelope nodded. "I understand."

"I'd rather be Blythe's friend, and have her in my life, than admit how I feel and hear her tell me there's no way she'll ever feel the same. I like her, Tiger. Really like her. I'm terrified of screwing this up somehow."

"Just be honest with her. I understand where you're coming from, but you're right, you're a hell of a man—and yeah, you're overbearing, overprotective, and annoyingly macho, just like the others." She smiled to let him know she was teasing. "Any woman, and especially Blythe, would be lucky to have you by her side. She's lived a hard life, Squirrel. I'm guessing she couldn't give a flying fuck about what a man looks like. She'll be more interested in what he's like on the inside. And you, my friend, are amazing. And from the little you've told me about her, exactly what she needs."

"Thanks, Tiger," Squirrel said. "I appreciate it."

"You need anything, all you gotta do is ask," she said.

"I know. And believe me, I won't hesitate to ask if I need you."

"Good. Now…did I tell you what Smokey did yesterday?"

Squirrel shook his head and didn't even feel bad when he tuned Penelope out. All she ever talked about lately was her new pet and how amazing he was. He'd heard so many stories about how "Smokey did this…" or "Smokey did that…" that he was donkey-ed out.

All he could think about was Blythe. He liked her. She was funny and, based on the stories she'd told him about helping out others on the street, genuinely nice. Squirrel worried about her constantly. The sooner Blythe was off the streets herself, the happier he'd be.

CHAPTER TWO

*B*lythe shoved the cell phone to the very bottom of her backpack and zipped it. She shivered, even though it wasn't cold outside. Looking around, she mentally sighed. She'd gotten to the shelter too late tonight to get a bed. She totally understood why Tadd had said he didn't like the shelters, but Blythe much preferred them over sleeping on the streets.

She'd thought her life was bad when she was living in the abandoned building with Tadd and his wife and dog, but she hadn't realized how good she'd had it. Living on the streets sucked. Majorly.

Part of it was boredom. There was literally nothing to do. Oh sure, she could walk around and look for money on the ground, or try to scope out safe places to sleep, but for someone who was used to being busy from the time she got up in the morning until she went to sleep, having nothing to do was almost painful.

But mostly, life on the streets sucked because she never felt safe. Ever. Probably because she *was* never safe. It was a dog-eat-dog world, and it seemed as if everyone she met was waiting for her to screw up.

And she'd screwed up a lot when she'd first found herself homeless. She'd trusted the wrong people and had all her belongings stolen. She'd thought she'd found a group of people she could hang around with—because there was safety in numbers on the streets— but they'd ended up being a bunch of thugs who found pleasure in robbing others.

She'd tried to use some of the services that were available for the homeless, especially homeless women, but so far nothing had worked out long term. She'd gotten some clothes and even had an interview arranged, but the night before, she couldn't get into the shelter and had to sleep under a trash bin. She'd missed her interview because she'd been trying to find a place to take a shower, without success.

Another time, her bag had been stolen while she'd been *in* the shower, and she'd had to cancel the interview once again. It seemed as if every time she tried to get help to get off the streets, something had transpired to keep her knocked down.

Some days, it took more effort to keep trying than to just succumb to the helplessness that seemed to permeate the air around the shelters and on the street.

Now, the closest she'd come to letting her guard down recently, and truly connecting with someone else on the streets, had been with Tadd and Louise. But they'd been hurt in the fire that had burned down their sanctuary.

That had also been the night she'd met Sawyer.

She'd seen him from across the road and had found herself heading toward him before she knew what she was doing. He'd reminded her of her very first boyfriend.

She'd been in the fourth grade and had the biggest crush on a little boy in her class. He was short, nerdy, wore glasses...and wanted nothing to do with her. All he was interested in was math and reading. At recess, he sat against the brick wall of the school and read. Blythe had tried to get him to play, but he'd ignored her. She'd had a crush on that kid for years. She'd never been attracted to the jocks and popular kids. There was just something about a guy who had a brain in his head that did it for her.

In high school, she'd dated the president of the

chess club, who was also the third-chair trumpet player. Matt was hilarious and smart, but there had still been something missing. Oh, he was generous and funny, but when they'd graduated from high school, she hadn't felt bad when he went off to the northeast to school and she'd stayed in San Antonio.

There had been something about Sawyer that had struck Blythe the moment she'd seen him. He was standing next to a fire truck and listening intently to the others around him. His gaze was fixed on the burning building as if it was talking to him. He'd pushed his glasses up on his nose a couple of times…and that had been that. She'd found herself leaving the corner she'd been hiding in and heading straight for him.

If anyone could help Sophie, Tadd, and Louise, she'd known it would be him.

He hadn't blown her off, had listened to what she'd told him—then surprisingly, had given her his sweatshirt because she was cold. Things had gotten crazy after that, and Blythe had done what she usually did, faded into the background. She'd seen her friends rescued and had watched as the sanctuary she'd been living in burned to the ground.

It wasn't until later, when she'd crawled under a bush in a park, that she realized there was something in the pocket of the sweatshirt she'd been given.

She'd pulled it out from under her and stared at the expensive phone in disbelief.

Her first thought was that she needed to return it. But the firefighters were long gone by then.

It had vibrated a few times that night with incoming messages and texts. Blythe had felt so guilty for having the phone. She hadn't stolen it, but she *felt* as if she had all the same. She figured that the firefighter would eventually deactivate the phone when he got a new one, but he hadn't.

Instead, he'd started texting her.

Squirrel: Hey, pretty lady.
   Squirrel: I'm Squirrel.
   Squirrel: Real name is Sawyer.
   Squirrel: You can keep the phone.
   Squirrel: 2-2-5-5 is the unlock code.

She couldn't believe that he was just giving her his phone. Figured there had to be more to it. But he continued to text her. Short little notes that Blythe found herself looking forward to seeing every day.

Finally, after a horrible day, and while she was lying in an alley, scared because she'd barely managed to hide from a group of thugs who'd wanted something she wasn't willing to give them, she'd caved, unlocked the firefighter's phone, and texted him back.

Squirrel: you're insane.

He'd texted back immediately.

Squirrel: Blythe! Finally! I thought you were never going to talk to me!

And that was that. They'd talked for an hour that night. She offered to leave his phone at the hospital for him, but he'd told her to keep it. They texted until the battery on the phone was almost drained dry. He'd walked her through how to change the name so it didn't look like he was texting himself. He'd told her she could charge the phone at any of the branches of the public library downtown. She'd teased him for some of the apps he had on the phone, and he'd teased her right back when she admitted she had no idea what Snapchat was.

By the end of the night, she'd felt almost normal.

Almost forgot that she was lying on the ground in a foul-smelling alley, hiding from a group of men who wanted to rape and probably kill her.

Over the last couple of months, the feeling of safety and contentment only increased every time she talked to Sawyer. It was as if talking to him kept her in a bubble of protection. She could pretend she was a normal woman, talking to a man she was interested in, and who was interested in her right back. But the second she hung up, reality was always a hard pill to swallow.

She *wasn't* normal. She was homeless. Living on the streets. Everything she owned was in the bag on her back. She smelled. She was dirty.

And she really needed to ditch the phone and stop torturing herself by talking to Sawyer.

But she couldn't. His phone was her lifeline. She'd used it several times to call the police when she'd witnessed things on the streets that she couldn't ignore. And she'd used it to call Sawyer to tell him what had happened to his friends.

Blythe still felt awful for her part in what had happened to Milena and her friend. Yes, her involvement had ensured a little boy had been returned to his mother safely, but it wasn't enough to assuage the guilt Blythe felt over telling a scary, psycho man where Milena was that night. He'd kidnapped

Milena and her friend. Luckily, Sawyer had told her they were both fine, but that didn't make Blythe feel any better.

And thoughts of Hope and her son Billy still tormented her. She hadn't seen them in way too long. She had no idea where they'd gone, and the thought that they might be hurt or in trouble was excruciatingly painful.

Things had been stilted in her texts with Sawyer tonight, and Blythe knew why. She knew he didn't like the fact that she was homeless. Hell, *she* didn't like it. But she couldn't accept his help. She should, she knew that, but she'd been burned in the past by someone who'd said he only wanted to help.

It was why she was on the streets in the first place.

But the more she got to know Sawyer, and the longer she was on the streets, the more she wanted to take him up on his offers. Would it be so bad to be in his debt? He wasn't like the landlord who had promised to work with her regarding the rent, but then got tired of waiting for her to catch up with what she owed him. He was honorable. He was *Sawyer*.

Blythe shifted on the hard concrete, trying to get comfortable. She was extremely sore tonight. She'd walked for what seemed like miles, looking for Hope and Billy, but hadn't had any luck in finding them. It seemed as if they'd fallen off the face of the earth. Now she was using her backpack as a pillow and had a piece of cardboard over her legs. She had wedged herself as far under the trash bin as possible, even though it stunk to high heaven. She'd found that, for the most part, people would leave her alone if she slept under the trash. The parks were the worst places to try to get a decent night's sleep, even though they were the cleanest.

She'd just closed her eyes when she heard a scream from the other end of the alley.

Blythe was immediately awake. She could no more ignore a scream of distress than she could ignore a crying baby or child.

Shifting slowly so she wouldn't make any noise, Blythe sat up. She unzipped her backpack and pulled out the phone she'd recently stashed. She dialed nine-one-one but didn't hit send. Not yet. She needed to see what was going on first. She sent a silent prayer of thanks to Sawyer once again for letting her have his phone. She wasn't sure she'd have the guts to check out what was happening without the reassurance that she could call the police and have them on their way within seconds.

Not willing to leave her belongings for even the minute or two it would take to investigate, Blythe shrugged the backpack onto her shoulders. Gripping the phone tightly in her hand, she eased down the alley toward where she could hear voices.

She'd decided to sleep in the more touristy part of downtown. It was risky, because while it might seem like it was the safer option, most nights it was dangerous from ten to two. The mentally unstable or simply bad people who hung out on the streets were more likely to try to rob or assault tourists for the money and jewelry they inevitably carried and wore.

Tonight was no exception.

At the entrance to the alley were two thugs Blythe knew well. They were part of the group that had chased her earlier that night. Dog and Tweek.

She had no idea what their real names were, but it didn't matter. Dog was probably in his mid-forties. He was a little taller than her own five-seven, and wiry. Every time she'd seen him, he was filthy. His hands were covered in black dirt and his clothes were always torn and tattered. He had a bushy black beard that hit him mid-chest. Blythe had been disgusted by his rotting teeth the one time he'd cornered her and smiled cruelly.

Tweek was newer to the area. When she was hiding from the group earlier, she'd heard some of the other men talking about him. Apparently, he was in his early twenties and had shown up one day with a ton of drugs he'd stolen from his dealer. He was hiding out on the streets and had joined Dog's group. They were happy to have him because it seemed he was able to charm some of the local prostitutes. The group had laughed at the memory of Tweek bringing the latest prostitute into an alley, and her horror when she realized that, instead of quickly servicing Tweek and making a few bucks, she was expected to service all five men.

Blythe shuddered, recalling what they'd done to the poor woman. It had made her all the more determined to get away from them—and to finally accept Sawyer's help. She was too aware it could easily be *her* on the ground in an alley, being raped by Dog, Tweek, and their cronies.

She'd been on the verge of telling him earlier when they'd been texting, but she knew if she'd said something, he'd immediately want to come and get her…and she was still just barely vain enough to not want him to see her after she'd been sleeping under the trash bin. She'd let him know tomorrow after she'd had a chance to clean up.

A low voice brought her out of her musings and made Blythe remember where she was.

"Leave her alone."

Dog laughed as he brandished a knife at the couple.

The man was wearing a gray suit and lavender tie to match his date's dress. He was standing in front of her, one arm stretched out, as if that alone could keep her safe. The woman was wearing a pair of high heels and her light purple dress came to mid-thigh. The purse she'd been carrying was lying on the ground in front of the couple, open. The man's wallet also lay on the ground. Dog and Tweek had obviously already gone through both and taken anything of value.

Blythe would've slipped away quietly at that point, even after seeing the look of lust on Tweek's face. He was standing about four feet behind Dog, licking his lips as if he were starving and someone had just placed a full plate of food in front of him.

But it was the look on the man's face that ultimately kept Blythe from leaving. Even from where she was standing nearly at the other end of the alley, she could see the desperation and fear. Not fear for himself, she was certain, but fear for the woman he was with.

He continued to keep himself between her and Dog and Tweek, trying to protect her. He was doing his best to back up, away from the danger, but every time he took a step, Tweek and Dog would close in, yelling at him to stay still.

Not even thinking about what being a snitch might mean for her if word got out that she'd been the one to call the cops, Blythe hit the send button on the phone. She kept her eyes on the situation in front of her as she quickly informed the dispatcher of what was happening and where they were. She clicked off the phone, even though she was instructed to stay on the line, and shoved it into the outer pocket of her backpack.

Knowing she needed to give the police some time to arrive, Blythe looked around frantically. She needed a distraction...and a weapon to protect herself. She knew without a doubt that Dog and Tweek weren't going to take her interference kindly.

Seeing what she needed, Blythe stepped out of the shadows.

The movement must've caught Dog's eyes, because she heard him shout, "There's that bitch!"

Blythe palmed the broken bottle with one hand and picked up a long piece of wood with the other. "Leave them alone," she called out, not moving toward them.

"Why don't you come here and make us?" Tweek yelled.

Time seemed to stand still. The tourist couple stood frozen at the mouth of the alley while Dog and Tweek divided their attention between them and Blythe.

Knowing she was going to piss them off, she yelled, "I've called the cops!"

"Fuck. Stupid bitch," Dog growled.

He looked at his partner and, as if they shared a brain, they turned away from the couple and headed down the alley toward her.

"Run!" Blythe screamed at the man and woman, who were standing stock still where they'd been the entire time. But her single word was enough to break the man from his trance, and he spun, keeping himself between his woman and the alley and hurrying her away from the danger.

Blythe had time to be thankful he hadn't tried to gather their belongings before fleeing. She'd seen idiots do just that. Show more concern over their material things than getting to safety.

As happy as she was that the couple had gotten away, even if she wished she had a man who would be willing to stand between her and danger the way the stranger had done, she now had to deal with a very pissed-off Dog and Tweek.

They were closing in on her quickly, and without taking her eyes from them, Blythe backed up. She was cornered in the dead-end alley, with nowhere to run. She tightened her hold on the bottle and the piece of wood, knowing they wouldn't protect her much but refusing to drop them.

"If you wanted some of this, all you had to do was ask, bitch," Tweek sneered as he palmed his dick.

Blythe wanted to gag but didn't say a word.

"Where'd you go earlier?" Dog asked as he continued to stalk her. "We wanted to play."

"Sorry, but I had better things to do," Blythe returned.

"What's better than a good fuck?" Tweek asked.

"I really have called the cops. You two better get on out of here before they get here," Blythe told them in desperation.

"We aren't afraid of no asshole pigs. But now that you mention it, maybe we *should* take this party somewhere else."

Blythe had no intention of going anywhere with them. If they took her from the alley, they'd inevitably bring her to where their buddies were hanging out, and she'd never get away from them. At least not before they hurt her. Badly.

"I think not."

"I think so." And with that, Dog nodded at Tweek —and they both rushed her.

Blythe let out a squeak of surprise at their sudden attack but didn't try to run. It was too late for that, and there was literally nowhere for her to go. She mentally prepared to do as much damage to them as possible before they incapacitated her.

She did her best, slicing Tweek across the cheek with the bottle before he got ahold of her. She writhed and squirmed in his hold, refusing to give up. She felt a sudden pain in her side but ignored it, knowing whatever they had planned for her would be much worse than a knife wound.

Screaming at the top of her lungs, Blythe fought for her life. She kicked and scratched and when Dog finally got her on the ground, even used her head to try to hit him.

Tweek managed to get control of her hands and he pinned her wrists to the ground over her head. Dog literally sat on her pelvis, keeping her immobile under him. Her back was arched because she still wore her backpack, and she thrashed under the two men, doing whatever she could to delay the inevitable.

Tweek's dirty palm covered her mouth and he leered at her.

"Shhhhh, bitch. You know you want this. All you bitches are in heat for a hard dick."

Blythe glared at him and tried not to hyperventilate. She couldn't breathe very well through her nose.

Dog was still holding the knife in his hand, and he ran the flat side of the blade down her neck. "Are you going to be a good girl?"

Blythe shook her head violently. They might rape her, but she wasn't going to make it easy for them. No way in hell.

One moment she was glaring up at Dog and Tweek, and the next, a pain so intense she couldn't think straight was shooting through her body.

She vaguely heard Dog laughing but couldn't concentrate on what he was doing.

"Do it again," Tweek ordered. "It takes the fight right out of her."

"What if I like a little fight?" Dog replied, but when he was done speaking, Blythe felt more excruciating pain in her other side.

She vaguely felt Dog's hands fumbling at her pants, but her mind couldn't comprehend what was happening. She felt torn in so many different directions. The pain in her sides was overriding almost everything else. She barely noticed when Tweek took his hand off her mouth and moved it to her chest.

"She's got a good set of tits on her," Tweek said as he cruelly pinched her nipples through her shirt.

It was the feel of Dog's hands on her lower belly that brought Blythe back to where she was and what was happening. If she didn't do something, she was going to be raped right here, right now. In a disgusting alley, as if she were nothing but a piece of trash.

Using all her strength, Blythe felt around for her makeshift weapons.

Her hand closed on the broken bottle and without thinking, she grabbed it and swung as hard as she could, stabbing Tweek in the neck.

Her hand slipped off the neck of the bottle as she hit Tweek, but the pain of the glass cutting into her own palm didn't even register.

Before she could go for Dog, his hands closed around her throat, cutting off all her air.

"You're going to regret doing that," he snarled. "You should've just laid there and let us take what we wanted. Stupid cunt! Now you're going to die right here like the trash you are. But you know what? Me and Tweek are still gonna fuck you. We'll take your cold, dead body and fuck you in every orifice. Then we'll bring you to our friends and let them do the same thing. No one will notice or care. You know why? Because you're *nobody*. No one gives a shit about you or you wouldn't be out here on the streets."

Blythe wanted to deny his words. Tell him that she *was* somebody. That she had friends who would miss her. Family who loved her. But it wasn't exactly true.

The sound of sirens suddenly blared through the night. It was hard to tell how close they were as the noise echoed off the tall buildings all around them.

Blythe closed her eyes, and the first thing that came to her mind right before she passed out was Sawyer. How he'd looked standing next to the fire truck, as if he could save the world.

She didn't need him to save the world, though. Just her.

CHAPTER THREE

S quirrel woke with a start when his cell phone rang. He looked around, getting his bearings. He was at the fire station. He'd fallen asleep in one of the recliners in the common area. The TV was still on, a show about women who killed their significant others playing in the background.

He looked down at his phone and was surprised to see Blythe's name on the screen.

Seeing the time, one-thirty in the morning, made Squirrel instantly uneasy. Blythe had told him more than once that she didn't like using his phone after ten because advertising that she had an expensive piece of equipment like a smartphone, after she went into the shelter for the night, was never a good idea.

He didn't hesitate to answer. "Hello?"

"Hello. Who is this?"

The question immediately irritated Squirrel. Whoever it was had called *him*, not the other way around. If someone had stolen the phone from Blythe, he was going to be pissed way the hell off. "Who are *you*, and why do you have Blythe's phone?"

"My name is Detective Bruce Nelson. There's been an incident."

Squirrel was already up and on the move before the detective's last statement. All he'd needed to hear was that there was a detective on the other end of the line.

"Where's Blythe?"

"We don't have an ID on the victim, but when we searched her belongings, we found this phone. And your number was the most recent one in her call list…other than 9-1-1."

Squirrel's stomach dropped and he stopped in the middle of the room, paralyzed.

He was a professional. He was the one people looked to in emergencies, but for some reason, hearing the word "victim" in relation to Blythe made him forget all his training. He didn't know what to do or what to say.

"Where is she?" he finally croaked out.

"She'll be brought to San Antonio Methodist Hospital. Do you know where that is?"

Squirrel nodded, not realizing the man on the other end of the phone couldn't see him. "Is she... how bad is she?"

"I'm not sure. You'll have to talk to the doctors at the hospital. I need to go. The ambulance is ready to leave. I'll put her phone and belongings in the ambulance with her."

And with that, the detective hung up.

Squirrel stood in the middle of the room and tried to get himself to move.

Blythe had been hurt. While he'd been sleeping, she'd been hurt.

"Squirrel? What's wrong?"

He turned toward the voice and saw Driftwood standing in the entrance to the hallway that led to the sleeping rooms.

"Blythe." It was all he could think to say. His mind was going in a thousand different directions. He couldn't even imagine what had happened to her. Didn't want to think about it. He'd seen a lot in his job as a paramedic/firefighter and didn't want to think about Blythe suffering like any of the victims he'd seen over the years.

Without a word, Driftwood disappeared into the hallway behind him. Within moments, he was back with Chief.

"What's wrong with Blythe?" Chief asked, coming up to his friend.

"I don't know. She...a detective called me. Said he found my phone. She's on her way to San Antonio Methodist."

Chief nodded and turned to Driftwood. "I'll get him ready. You tell Sledge where we're going. I'll call Sophie on the way."

Squirrel knew he should be doing something, but he felt as if he were trapped in a vat of peanut butter. Moving was hard, thinking was harder.

"Squirrel...snap out of it, man," Chief told him sternly. "Blythe needs you. You gonna stand here all night?"

Blinking, Squirrel looked up at his friend. "No."

"Good. Then put your boots on and let's get the fuck out of here."

As if his words were a cold shower, Squirrel snapped out of whatever funk he'd been in. He needed to get to Blythe. Now. She was hurt and headed to the hospital. He needed to make sure she got the care she needed. There were a million other things he needed to do, but first and foremost was getting to Blythe.

He turned and grabbed his boots and shoved his feet into them. By the time he was finished lacing them up, Driftwood and Chief were standing by the door. As he walked to Chief's pickup, he asked, "Sledge okay with us leaving?"

"Yeah," Driftwood said. "He's already calling in replacements."

Nodding, Squirrel settled into the front seat as Chief started his truck and peeled out of the parking lot. "Can I still bring Blythe to Sophie's old house?" Squirrel asked the large Native American.

"Of course."

"And Blythe will need stuff. Clothes, girly shit. That kind of stuff," Squirrel mumbled.

"I'll have Crash talk to Adeline. I'm sure she'll mobilize the other women," Driftwood piped up from the backseat.

Squirrel nodded.

"Did the detective say what happened?" Chief asked.

"No. Just that he found my phone in her back-pack and she was on her way to the hospital."

As if he could hear the panic in Squirrel's tone, Chief said, "Easy, man. Don't borrow trouble."

Chief was right, but Squirrel couldn't help but think the worst. And beat himself up. "I should've done something before now. I knew she was on the streets, but I let her talk me out of helping her. I'm such an idiot."

"You're not an idiot," Driftwood said. "As much as

we want to save the world sometimes, we can't always do it. Especially not when the woman we want to protect won't let us."

Squirrel knew exactly what his friend was referring to. Driftwood had been attracted to Quinn Dixon, one of Sophie's friends, since the moment he'd lain eyes on her, but she didn't seem interested in pursuing anything with him. The only thing keeping him from pursuing her more aggressively was the fact Sophie had told him Quinn wasn't interested in a relationship with *anyone*. It wasn't him, per se. She had no self-esteem because of the port-wine birthmark on her face, and she'd had enough bad experiences with men that she was leery of anyone who showed her the least amount of attention.

"It's not the same," he told Driftwood in a soft voice. "It's not a matter of me taking my time and wooing her. She was in danger every minute of every day, and I did *nothing*. I had Beth track her down, but I refused to let her tell me where she was because I knew Blythe wanted to get back on her feet on her own. I could've given her money, made her meet with Tadd and Louise, had Sophie invite her to live in her vacant house before now. But I didn't!"

"Stop it," Chief ordered. "Regret is an appalling

waste of energy. You can't build on it; it's only good for wallowing in."

Squirrel pondered his friend's words for a moment. He was right. He couldn't go back and change the past, but he sure as hell could change the future. "You're right. I appreciate your Navajo wisdom, Chief."

Chief barked out a laugh. "That wasn't Navajo. Katherine Mansfield said that."

"Who's that?"

"She was a short-story writer from New Zealand. She died at age thirty-four, but I've found many jewels of wisdom in her words."

Squirrel merely shook his head. Chief was an interesting man. At times spouting mystical beliefs and other times swearing like a sailor. He was a contradiction, and he loved him like a brother.

"I'm going to pull up in front. You two go in and see what you can find out. Sophie's on her way. If no one will talk to you, she'll make sure you get the info you need."

Squirrel had wanted to tell Chief not to bother Sophie, but he was selfish enough to want her there, just in case. She worked at the lab next door to the hospital and knew most of the doctors and staff. If he couldn't get any information, she'd be able to for sure.

He nodded and turned his attention back to Blythe. He needed to see her. Needed to make sure she was all right. Things were going to be different from here on out. It didn't matter what happened to put her on the streets, she was about to find out what kind of friend he was. The kind who did the right thing—regardless of whether she wanted him to or not.

CHAPTER FOUR

*B*lythe came back to consciousness suddenly. One minute she was out, the next she was fully aware. Instead of opening her eyes right away, however, she stayed perfectly still and tried to figure out where she was and why she hurt so badly.

Recollections of what had happened came back when she heard someone speaking beside her.

"Three knife wounds to the upper torso. None look to be life threatening. Her hand is still bleeding pretty badly though. Her BP and vitals are good. Looks like she'll need a few stitches in each of the knife wounds and a dozen or so in her palm. ETA is about ten minutes. Oh, and warn the staff that she smells pretty rank. Looks like she's been living on the streets for a while. Out."

Blythe tried not to be offended by the man's observation. She did stink. She knew it, but it wasn't as if she could do much about it. There were showers at the shelter but they weren't safe to use, as there was no place to put her belongings while she showered; she'd learned that the hard way. There had been incidents of assault while women were showering as well.

No, she'd rather be smelly than risk losing everything she owned and being raped in the shelter.

She opened her eyes and stared at the paramedic hovering above her.

"Hang in there," he said gently. "We'll be at the hospital before you know it."

"I don't have any money," Blythe told him, wanting to make that perfectly clear, as if it wasn't already.

The young man patted her hand and said, "I figured. It's okay."

Blythe closed her eyes. She didn't know how it would be okay, but she didn't have the energy to worry about it.

Then another thought hit her. Her eyes popped open and she tried to lift her head to look around, but she was strapped to a gurney and couldn't move. "My things! Where's my backpack?"

"Relax, it's here. One of the detectives brought it over before we left."

Blythe let out a sigh of relief. One backpack might not mean much to the man sitting next to her, but to her, it was the world. Besides, it held her phone…and the only way to connect to Sawyer.

With that thought in her head, Blythe relaxed and let the painkillers she'd been given do their thing.

She woke up when the gurney was removed from the back of the ambulance with a jerk. She kept quiet as she was wheeled into the emergency entrance and into an open room. Within moments, a nurse appeared above her and set about releasing her from the backboard she was Velcroed to.

She was assisted into a hospital gown and covered up by a sheet before the nurse left, saying a doctor would be in as soon as possible.

Looking around, Blythe saw her backpack sitting on the floor against a wall, and again sighed in relief. The drugs in her system made her feel pretty mellow, but the wounds in her body still throbbed.

Thinking about what happened, Blythe realized she'd been extremely lucky. Dog and Tweek had almost raped her. She swallowed hard, feeling the tightness in her throat where she'd nearly been strangled. If the police had been even a few minutes later, she would've been dead. She knew it as clearly as she knew her own name.

Just as she knew things weren't over between her and her attackers. She'd hurt Tweek pretty badly. She'd felt the glass from the bottle sink into his neck before her hand had slipped off the bottle. He wouldn't be happy about that. And he and Dog would go back to their little gang of friends and tell them what had happened, as well.

They'd be looking for her. The second she stepped foot back on the streets, she'd have a target on her back. Even staying in the shelter wouldn't be safe, Blythe knew.

She sighed, this time in frustration. She was tired, hurting, and scared.

Then, when she heard the nurses talking outside her room, added humiliated to the list of things she was feeling. Their voices were lowered, and they probably thought she was still out of it, but she heard every demeaning word.

"God, I don't know how you could stand to be in there with her."

"Right? You think it stinks out here...I had to hold my breath when I helped her out of her shirt. Lord."

"You gonna warn Doctor Adams?"

"I don't need to. The second he steps foot on the

floor, he'll know we've got another homeless patient. They always stink things up in here so bad, it takes almost a whole can of disinfectant spray to get it halfway back to normal."

Blythe's eyes filled with tears. The nurses weren't saying anything that wasn't true, but it still hurt. She'd done her best to stay clean, but it was almost impossible when she had to sleep under trash bins and in the smelliest corners of the city.

She lay there feeling sorry for herself for a while —how long she had no idea, since there was no clock in the room and she didn't have a watch— when she was startled by several raised voices in the hallway.

"Where is she?"

"Sir, you can't go back there."

"It's okay, Heather, he's with m-me."

"Sophie, I don't think—"

"He's with m-me," the woman named Sophie repeated firmly. "Where is s-she?"

"Room ten. Just follow the smell," the nurse said waspishly.

Before Blythe could blink, the door to her room opened all the way and a man and a woman entered.

Blythe knew at first glance it was Sawyer. She recognized him from when she'd met him at the fire, but since, she'd also examined every photo on his old phone. It was more than obvious who he was.

"Blythe!" he exclaimed as he came toward her.

Feeling self-conscious about her lack of proper clothing, and because of the conversation she'd over-heard, she blurted, "Don't!"

Sawyer stopped in his tracks. "Don't what?"

"Don't come any closer. I know I smell. I can't help it."

"Fucking nurses," Sawyer said under his breath, and then he took the two steps required to bring him to her side. He picked up her uninjured hand and wrapped his fingers around hers.

The warmth coming from his palm was amazing. But it was the feeling of being touched, gently, that made Blythe lose it. It had been so long since someone had touched her. Touched her in a nice way, that was.

The tears welled up from deep inside her and spilled down her cheeks as if a faucet had been turned on full blast.

Instead of telling her to hush, Sawyer brought her hand up to his lips and gently kissed her filthy knuckles. "You're okay, baby. You're okay."

Blythe cried harder. She cried for her mom. She cried because she'd lost all her belongings when her landlord changed the locks on her apartment and threw her stuff on the curb, where it was picked through by strangers then rained on before she could find the means to store it. She cried for all the nights she'd been scared and for all the times she'd wanted to simply give up.

But mostly, she cried because it had been so long since anyone had looked at her with as much compassion and tenderness as Sawyer was now.

After a while, she tried to get herself under control. "Great," she mumbled. "Now I stink and have snot running down my face."

Sawyer smiled at her. "It's not all that bad."

Blythe rolled her eyes. "Liar. Even the cockroaches don't want anything to do with me."

"I'm s-sorry you had to hear that, Blythe."

Blythe turned her head to look at the woman who had entered the room with Sawyer. Sophie. Now that she had a chance to really look at her, she recognized her right away. She'd been so kind to her, Tadd, and Louise before the building they'd been living in had burned down, always bringing them muffins and coffee. "Hi, Sophie."

"Hi," the other woman returned. "I'm s-sorry you got hurt."

"Thanks."

"I heard Doctor Adams will be looking at you. He's good. He'll fix you up in no time."

Blythe nodded, not really sure what to say.

"Detective Nelson will be on his way here to get your statement too," Sawyer informed her.

Blythe frowned.

"What?"

It wasn't that she didn't want to tell the cops what had happened, but she knew it wouldn't keep her safe. Dog and Tweek would get to her again, no matter what the police said or did. "Nothing. That's fine."

Sawyer eyed her for a long moment, then turned to Sophie. "Thanks for getting me in here. We'll be good for a while."

Sophie nodded. "Great. I'll just go and take care of what we talked about."

"Thanks, Soph."

"It's good to s-see you again, Blythe. I'm only s-sorry it's under these circumstances."

"Me too," Blythe told her honestly. She'd always liked Sophie. She seemed a bit naïve and too nice, if there was such a thing, but she liked her all the same. "Bye."

Sophie gave her a distracted wave as she headed out of the small room. She was already looking down at her cell phone and her thumbs were in motion as she typed and walked at the same time.

"Hi," Blythe said nervously as she looked up at Sawyer.

He smiled and squeezed her hand. "Hi. It's nice to formally meet you. I'm Sawyer McClay. My friends call me Squirrel."

Blythe's lips quirked. "I'm Blythe Coopman. It's nice to meet you. And if it's all the same to you, I'd prefer to call you Sawyer."

"You can call me anything you want." He let go of her hand and sat in the bedside chair, then leaned over, supporting himself with his elbows on the edge of the mattress. "What happened?"

Blythe sighed. "In a nutshell, these two guys were robbing a couple. I called nine-one-one and intervened."

Sawyer frowned at her. "That wasn't smart."

"I know that," Blythe retorted. "But was I supposed to ignore it? Let them get hurt or killed? I mean, I hadn't planned on making a trip to the ER tonight. But there I was, trying to sleep under my trash can, and I couldn't help but hear Dog and Tweek yelling at the poor couple, whose only crime was probably trying to walk to their car after seeing a show."

"Fuck," Sawyer swore as he leaned back in his chair. His head tilted up so he was looking at the ceiling, giving Blythe an unencumbered view of his

Adam's apple and corded neck. A neck she wanted to lean forward and lick.

She chuckled at the inappropriate thought.

Sawyer's head came down and his eyes narrowed as he gazed at her. "What the hell can be funny right about now?"

She shrugged, biting her lip to keep her thoughts to herself.

Sawyer continued to look pissed for a second, but then his lips quirked up into a grin. "It's impossible to stay in a bad mood around you. How much painkiller did they give you?"

Blythe shrugged again.

"I'm sorry you were hurt, baby. I'm so sorry."

"Baby…?"

"Sorry. It just keeps popping out."

Maybe it was the drugs, but she secretly liked the term of endearment. "I'm sorry I was hurt too," Blythe told him. "But you know what?"

"What?"

"They got away."

"Who? The thugs who dared to touch you?"

Blythe shook her head. "No. The couple. He was so protective of her. You know that song by Tim McGraw?" Her voice was a bit slurred from the drugs as she spoke.

"Which song?" Sawyer's voice was low and even. He didn't take his eyes from hers.

Blythe wrinkled her brows, trying to think of the name of it and having a hard time concentrating. "It starts out with a boy mad at his dad for letting the girl next door come on a fishing trip with them... um... Oh! I know! *Don't Take The Girl*. That's the one."

"Yeah, baby, I know the song."

"It was as if the man were the living embodiment of that song. You know, the part when the couple is held up and he begs the guy not to take his girlfriend?"

"I've heard it."

Blythe sighed. "He was so upset for his girlfriend or wife or whatever. Keeping his body between her and Dog and Tweek. The woman looked more pissed than scared, but still. You think she's okay?"

Blythe didn't even register Sawyer's touch on her arm as he spoke. She was thinking too hard about the couple.

"I'm sure she is."

"Good."

They were interrupted by a voice from the doorway. "I'm Doctor Adams. You're Blythe Coopman?"

"Last time I checked, yeah," she said, rolling her head because it was too heavy to pick up to look at the doctor as he entered. He was wearing a long white coat and had a stethoscope around his neck. "You look like a doctor," she blurted.

Doctor Adams chuckled. "It's a good thing, since I am one." He looked at Sawyer. "I'm going to have to ask you to step out."

Blythe gripped Sawyer's arm with her good hand and shook her head. "No. Please. Let him stay?"

The doctor looked between Sawyer and Blythe for a long moment, assessing. Then he nodded. "You're a friend of Sophie's, right?"

"Yes, sir," Sawyer responded. "And I'm a fire-fighter. Station 7. This isn't our normal route but I was here when the building next door burned down. I know this is unusual, but Blythe's family isn't around and she's scared. She was assaulted tonight, and I don't want her to feel alone."

"You're sure you want him to stay?" the doctor asked Blythe. "We'll need to discuss your health history. Are you okay with him hearing that?"

Blythe nodded. "It's fine."

The doctor stepped up to the side of the bed that Sawyer wasn't sitting on. He reached for the sheet. "All right then, let's take a look and see what the damage is, yeah?"

* * *

Squirrel clenched his teeth and barely held himself together as the doctor examined and treated Blythe. The first thing he'd seen when her gown had been lifted was the scratch marks on her lower belly. Compared to the three knife wounds on her upper torso, the scratches were negligible—but he saw them for what they were.

The asshole who'd hurt her had tried to get her pants off. His filthy hands had scratched the hell out of her belly.

He took a huge breath through his nose to try to control himself, the smell from Blythe reminding him of her situation...and his lack of action.

She'd been sleeping with the trash. He didn't give a shit about the smell. He could take care of that quickly enough. But the wounds she'd suffered wouldn't disappear as easily.

"It looks like the knife wounds should heal pretty well," the doctor told her as he took off his gloves. He'd just stitched her up and was giving her follow-up care instructions. "They weren't terribly deep. You were lucky. That wound on your hand needs to be watched, though. Don't use it, if at all possible. And it should be kept wrapped and clean for at least two weeks."

Blythe nodded.

"I'll write you a prescription for painkillers. Use them. Don't try to be a hero," he scolded.

Squirrel saw Blythe's eyes shift to the right, then back to the doctor's. "Okay."

He sighed, knowing she had no intention of filling the prescription. How could she? With no insurance and probably no money, she didn't have the means to do so.

"I'll take care of it, Doc," Squirrel told the other man.

Without pause, Doctor Adams nodded. "Good. There's a detective waiting outside to talk to you, if you're feeling up to it."

"Do I have a choice?" Blythe asked, her words almost slurring.

"Yes, you have a choice," Squirrel answered. "If you're too tired or can't deal with it tonight, you can do it tomorrow."

"But it's already tomorrow, isn't it?"

He refrained from rolling his eyes, barely. "Yeah, technically it is."

"I...I'll see him now. I don't know when I might have a chance to get to the station to talk to him."

Squirrel heard the doctor leaving but didn't spare him a glance. He sat on the bed at Blythe's hip and leaned over her. He put his hands on the mattress on either side of her shoulders and gazed down at her.

Her short dark hair was cut unevenly and was dirty and disheveled. She had smudges of blood on her cheek and there were dark circles under both eyes. She was pale, dirty, disheveled…and the pain in her hazel eyes made him want to pick her up and hold her close. From what he'd seen earlier, she was too skinny for her frame. He wanted to take care of that for her…make sure she had the nutrition she needed to get healthy.

But first, he needed to make sure she understood what was happening next.

"You're moving into Sophie's old house," he informed her, ignoring the way she opened her mouth to protest. "And I'm not letting you say no. She hasn't lived there since she moved in with Chief. It's right next door to them, though, so if you need anything, they're right there. Tadd and Louise moved out not too long ago. They'd been living there while they got back on their feet after the fire. If it was okay for them, why isn't it okay for you to do the same?"

Blythe stared up at him, clearly at a loss for words.

Moving one hand to brush a short lock of hair off her forehead, Squirrel continued, "It's clean, in a safe neighborhood, and close to the fire station where I work. I let you convince me you were okay on the streets for way too long. The truth is, it's *not* safe. Or healthy. And you know it.

"I like you, Blythe Coopman. A lot. And I can't spend one more night worrying about you. Wondering if you're hungry, cold, or safe. When I got that call from the detective tonight, the first thing I thought was that I was too late. That I'd dicked around too long and I'd never get the chance to really get to know you. I'm not dicking around anymore."

He stared down at her, daring her with his eyes to defy him. Wanting her to try. She didn't disappoint him.

"I'm not your responsibility."

"You're right, you're not. You're an adult who has taken care of herself for a long time. But you're my friend. And friends don't let friends sleep under trash bins if they can do something about it."

Blythe licked her lips and closed her eyes. "I can't think straight."

"Good," Squirrel countered smugly. Then he gentled his tone. "Please, Blythe. If you won't do it for yourself, do it for me."

She looked up at him. "Why? Why would you want to help me? I'm nobody. Just another homeless woman on the street. I could be a whore, earning my money on my back. A druggie. I could steal Sophie blind if I stayed at her house."

"But you're not a whore, a druggie, or a thief," Squirrel insisted. "And you're not *nobody*. You're Blythe Coopman. You're the woman who could've spent thousands of dollars buying stuff when I gave you the code to my phone. I've got passwords stored in there for all sorts of websites. But you didn't. The only people you've called are me, and the police now and then, and you've texted back and forth with my sisters."

Her eyes widened and she opened her mouth, but nothing came out.

His tone gentled. "Yeah, baby, I know about my sisters texting you. And I'm okay with that. My mom told me that Natalie was inconsolable after the boy she liked didn't call her when he said he would. But after you texted with her, she was okay again. Your perspective on which boy Charlotte should let take her to the school dance was right on. And you were one of the first to congratulate Emma when she found out about that scholarship she won. They've been bugging me to bring you over to the house."

"I'm sorry if I overstepped. I guess they didn't know about your other number, or forgot or something... But Natalie was so upset that first time she texted, I couldn't let her think you were ignoring her. H-How did you know I've been talking with them and why would you be okay with it?"

He didn't hide the truth. "First off, I'm close with my sisters. Emma and I have talked about what college she should go to and which have the best pre-med programs. Charlotte is her opposite; all she wants to do is play her flute...in college and beyond. Natalie couldn't care the least bit about academics right now...which boy might like her is all she's interested in these days. My point is, they tell me almost everything. And they told me all about how awesome you were, and they want to know when they're going to get to meet you in person.

"Secondly, Beth, my friend's woman, is a master hacker. The second she learned I'd lost my phone, she tracked it. Then she hacked into it again once you finally used my passcode. When you wouldn't let me help you, I told her to stop spying on you, but she still gave me weekly updates on who you were calling, texting, and what websites you were visiting, even though I asked her to quit. And lastly..."

Squirrel hesitated, but wanted to get it all out there now so she wouldn't have a reason to get pissed at him and leave later.

"Every picture you've taken has been stored in my cloud."

This time, Blythe closed her eyes and turned her

head to the side, as if trying to pretend she didn't hear him.

Squirrel put a hand on the side of her neck, his thumb brushing against her cheek. "They're beautiful and sad at the same time. You have an eye for really bringing the emotion out in a simple picture. A child's dirty hand, the food slopped onto a tray at the shelter, the rows upon rows of bunk beds in the shelter, a piece of cardboard lying under a trash bin ready to be slept on…they're heartbreaking and eye-opening at the same time.

"But not one picture you took makes me think less of you, baby. If anything, they make me more impressed. I can't imagine what you've been through, but I'm here now. Let me help you. Let Sophie help. No strings attached. I promise."

Her eyes stayed closed as she asked, "Will you stay with me when I talk to the detective?"

"Absolutely."

"Does Sophie's house have a shower?"

"Of course. I think it's got two."

She opened her eyes and looked up into his. "Will you ask the doctor if it's okay for me to get my stitches wet? I'd kill for a hot shower where I don't have to worry about anyone walking in on me or stealing my stuff while I'm preoccupied."

Squirrel let out the breath he'd been holding.

He'd been prepared to take her to Sophie's by force if he had to. But she'd given in.

He moved without thought. Leaning close, his mouth brushed hers in a barely there caress. "You got it, baby. You can stand in the shower until your skin wrinkles up so badly, you'll think you're an eighty-year-old woman. I have it on good authority that the hot water tank in Sophie's house is huge. You won't regret this," Squirrel added softly.

"I just hope *you* won't."

"Never. This day's been too long in coming. The only thing I regret is not getting to you sooner."

"I should've let you help me before now. I was stubborn, and it seems so stupid now," she told him.

They stared at each other for a heartbeat, until the moment was interrupted by a low, irritated voice from the hall.

"Goddamn, it stinks in here."

Pissed off on Blythe's behalf, Squirrel stood and crossed his arms over his chest. He stood by the side of the bed as if he were a sentry.

Within seconds, a police officer stuck his head in the door. "This the homeless woman who was assaulted?"

"You better check that attitude, Kirkpatrick," Squirrel threatened. He knew the officer, had met him a few times at various emergency calls they'd been at together.

"Hey, Squirrel. You find her and bring her in?"

"No. I'm her friend. And she has a name. It's Blythe. And if I hear one more derogatory word from your mouth, I'll be talking to your supervisor."

The detective looked taken aback for a moment before recovering. "Sorry. No offense intended." Then he looked at Blythe. "I'm sorry for what happened to you, ma'am. Are you ready to give your statement?"

Squirrel slowly sat in the chair he'd vacated and put his hand on Blythe's arm, offering his encouragement. He saw the tears in her eyes, but she blinked them away before she looked at the officer. "I'm ready."

Twenty minutes later, Blythe had finished recounting what had happened and how she'd ended up stabbed several times and lying in the emergency room. Squirrel wanted to find the assholes nicknamed Dog and Tweek and pound the shit out of them. Ask *them* how it felt to be on the receiving end of an ass beating...but Blythe needed him more.

She was obviously shaken up but trying to hide it. She was tired and hurting, and Squirrel needed to get her to Sophie's house. He'd touch base with his cop friends, Quint and TJ, later. The police were always patrolling the downtown areas for crime and trying to monitor the homeless population that lived down there. But panhandling and begging for food and money were one thing. Assault and battery, and attempted rape, were something else.

"You ready to go?" Squirrel asked Blythe after the detective had left.

She nodded.

"Let me help you." Squirrel lifted her easily when she started to sit up. She winced, but otherwise didn't complain.

He called for a nurse and turned his back when she helped Blythe back into her jeans and shirt. After the nurse left, and she was finally ready to go, her eyes went to her backpack in the corner and, without a word, Squirrel took the few steps to it and picked it up.

His eyebrows shot up in surprise. It was a lot heavier than he'd thought it would be.

"What do you have in here, rocks?" he teased.

Without smiling, Blythe said, "Everything I own."

That wiped the humor off his face fast enough. "Will you let me carry it for you?"

Squirrel knew what he was asking. He wanted her trust. Wanted her to let him take care of her, even if only by carrying her possessions. If she balked, he wouldn't push. He had plenty of time to gain her trust. He hoped.

She hesitated and stared at him for almost an entire minute.

Refusing to break the silence, Squirrel let her think it over.

He was rewarded when he saw her swallow hard, then say, "Okay. But please…be careful with it."

Squirrel didn't break eye contact as he shrugged the backpack onto one shoulder. He didn't care that it was covered in dirt or that it smelled a little funky. "I will. You, and this pack, won't be out of my sight until we get you home."

"Home," she whispered and swayed on her feet. "It's been so long since I've thought of anywhere as home."

"Come on," Squirrel told her, wrapping an arm around her waist and taking much of her weight. "Let's get going."

She let him lead her out of the room. The doctor had popped in after the detective left and given him the prescriptions for painkillers and antibiotics that Blythe needed. She'd signed discharge papers, and had either ignored or not seen the part where it said the bill had already been paid in full. Sophie had come through for him. Ensuring she got the discount for people without insurance and taking care of the bill on his behalf. He'd pay her back as soon as he could arrange it.

"How's your hand?" he asked as they walked.

"Fine."

"And your sides?"

"Good."

Squirrel rolled his eyes. He needed to work on her being more honest with him. He steered her down a short hallway and through a set of double doors that led into the waiting room.

Blythe stopped in her tracks at the sight that greeted them. The double doors knocking together as they closed behind them couldn't be heard above the noise in the room.

Everyone stopped speaking and turned to face them when they realized they were there.

Squirrel had hoped Blythe would be pleased, but instead, she turned to face him, buried her head in his chest, and burst into tears.

CHAPTER FIVE

*B*lythe couldn't hold back the tears when she saw everyone in the waiting room. She usually had much better control over her emotions, but everything that had happened tonight, plus the painkillers coursing through her body, had lowered her resistance.

"Shhhh," Sawyer consoled her as she continued to cry.

She felt his hand on her hair, holding her to him, but couldn't seem to stop bawling like a baby.

"Is she all right?"

"What's wrong?"

"Is she in pain? You need to get her home, Squirrel."

Blythe heard the questions directed at the man she was clinging to as if he were a buoy in a turbulent sea, and the only thing holding her up, but she couldn't seem to let go of him or lift her head to reassure everyone she was okay.

But she didn't need to. Sawyer had it covered.

"She's fine. Overwhelmed, I think."

Blythe struggled to bring herself under control. She took a deep breath, noticing how amazing Sawyer smelled as she did so. His clean, soapy scent reminded her of how unclean *she* smelled. And she was plastered to him from chest to hips.

She forced herself to take a step away and reached up to swipe at the tears on her face. But Sawyer got there before she did. Tenderly using his thumbs to brush against her cheeks.

He confused her to no end, but she couldn't deny there was something between them. All those late-night phone calls and marathon text sessions had forged a bond so strong, that finally being face-to-face only solidified it.

"You good?"

"I'm good," she whispered back, then, taking a deep breath, she turned around.

The room was full of people. At least it seemed that way to Blythe. She recognized everyone, even if she didn't know all their names.

Tadd and Louise were there, and of course Sophie. A Native American man was standing next to her with his arm around her waist. Blythe assumed that was Chief.

She recognized one of the women who worked at the same lab as Sophie. Quinn, she thought her name was. She was easy to remember because of the birthmark on her face. She'd also brought her and Tadd coffee more than once when they were living in the abandoned building next to the hospital.

Then there were all the people she'd only seen in the pictures on Sawyer's phone. A petite woman with black hair that matched the fur on the Labrador retriever sitting calmly at her side. A woman about Blythe's height, with long brown hair, who honestly looked like she wanted to be anywhere but there. She also had a dog at her side, wearing a service vest. It looked like it was part pit bull, but mostly mutt.

And then there were the men. She mentally counted. Seven, not including Sawyer. Blythe could tell immediately which were taken, as they stood next to their women, most touching them in some way. She also knew they were Sawyer's firefighting friends, as she'd seen all of them in his picture gallery on his phone.

No one said anything until a woman—even smaller than the one with the black dog—stepped forward. One of the tallest men in the room hovered right by her side. Blythe was almost amused at the height difference between them. It had to be at least a foot. She was concentrating so hard on placing all of the people, she almost missed what the blonde said.

"Hi, Blythe. I'm Penelope. I'm a friend of Squirrel's. We all are. We're so sorry you were hurt tonight. Are you okay?"

Blythe stared at everyone, one by one, and tried to wrap her brain around why they were there.

She felt Sawyer bend close a split second before she felt his warm breath waft over the side of her face as he spoke in her ear. "My parents would've brought my sisters, but I figured since they have school tomorrow, they could wait and see for themselves later that you're all right."

Looking up at Sawyer, Blythe blurted, "I don't understand. Why are they all here?"

The big man at Penelope's side answered her question. "Because you're Squirrel's friend. And any friend of his is a friend of ours. Besides, do you think we were going to pass up the chance to meet the woman who has our buddy wrapped around her little finger? No way."

"I noticed that you generally preferred to stay away from the River Walk area. Probably smart, too many people. At first, I didn't understand why you don't stay at the shelters every night, but after researching, I realized that they fill up really fast, and it's first come, first serve. That sucks." This from the uneasy-looking woman.

Blythe blinked. She knew this had to be Beth, the hacker. Embarrassed that she'd brought up the fact that she was living on the streets in front of everyone, Blythe wasn't sure what to say.

The man next to Beth put his hand on the back of her neck and said, "Not sure Blythe appreciates you throwing it in her face that she was homeless, honey."

Beth turned to look up at him. "I wasn't throwing it in her face. I was just making conversation." Her gaze swung back to Blythe's. "I'm impressed with how much ground you can cover in a day. If you were wearing a fitness tracker, you'd probably clock in twenty-thousand steps a day or more."

Blythe couldn't help but smile. She was still embarrassed as hell, but Beth made it seem like there was nothing wrong with trudging all over the city, looking for a safe place to crash.

Sophie came forward, with her man behind her, and said, "I'm s-so glad you're going to s-stay at m-my house. Everything's ready for you. S-Sheets are clean, towels washed, and tomorrow I'll go to the s-store and s-stock up the fridge for you. Is there anything in particular you want?"

"Uh…" Blythe's mind was blank. She hadn't thought about shopping in forever. Hell, finding something to eat usually meant suffering through whatever was served at the shelters or foraging through the trash bins she slept under.

Louise pushed through the growing crowd around Blythe and Squirrel and didn't even hesitate. She pulled Blythe forward and gave her a giant hug. They stood together like that for a long moment before Louise pulled back and turned to Sophie. "Whatever you get is fine. I'm guessing that Blythe isn't picky. Besides, it's too overwhelming to try to think about specifics when it's been forever since you got to choose your own food." She turned to face Blythe again. "I'm so glad to see you, honey. I'm sorry you were hurt. But you're safe now."

"I'm not sure about this," Blythe whispered to the old friend she never really expected to see again.

"I know you aren't. Tadd and I felt the same way. We'd been on our own for so long, we almost forgot what it was like to lean on someone else. To have friends who would have our back. I never used to think twice about my friends doing things for me, but after I was homeless, it felt too much like pity, so I stupidly turned away everyone's offer of help. Is that what happened with you?"

Blythe gave the older woman a small nod.

"Right. It'll take a while to figure out who you are again. As you know, when you're on the streets, the only thing you can think about is food, shelter, and safety. But one day soon, after you've been under a solid roof for a while, safe, eating healthy food, you'll realize that the people around you aren't helping because it's required of them, or because they want something from you. It's because they're truly good people and they genuinely *like* you."

Blythe's eyes filled with tears again. She was overwhelmed, and it was hard to believe she'd gone from sleeping under a trash can earlier that night to having over a dozen people hanging out at the hospital, waiting to see if she was all right.

"Okay, everyone, party's over," Sawyer announced to the group.

Blythe felt his hand touch lightly on her lower back. He wasn't pushing her. Wasn't trying to get her to move. He was just standing behind her, letting her know he was there. She felt herself leaning against that hand. Wanting to feel his comforting touch.

As if he could read her mind, Sawyer flattened his palm against her, giving her the support she craved.

"I'm going to take Blythe home. Sledge, will you talk to the chief and see if he can rearrange my shifts?"

"Already done," the man next to Beth said. "Before we went off duty this morning, we cleared it for you."

"Thanks. Crash, can you get ahold of TJ and let him know I'd like to speak with him? Maybe Quint too?"

"Of course."

"Driftwood?"

Blythe almost laughed when, after a prolonged silence, everyone turned to look at one of Sawyer's firefighting friends. He obviously hadn't heard Sawyer call his name—all his attention was on Sophie's friend, Quinn, who was studiously avoiding looking at him as if her life depended on it.

"Driftwood!" Sawyer repeated.

His friend's head whirled around and he stared at him. "What?"

"Geez. You need to stop fucking around," Sawyer said under his breath. Then louder, asked, "Will you and Taco go with Sophie to the store tomorrow? She'll need help with the bags."

Blythe looked up at Sawyer just in time to see him wiggling his brows at his friends. She almost rolled her eyes. He was so obvious.

"They're going to buy way too much food, aren't they?" she asked quietly.

"Of course they are," Louise answered her. "Just as they did when me and Tadd moved in."

Blythe opened her mouth to protest, but it was Tadd who interrupted before she could say a word.

"Let them," he ordered. "Let them take care of you, sweetheart. I should've insisted you come with us when we left, but by the time I realized what was happening, me and Louise were in the hospital and you were long gone. There's nothing wrong with accepting help."

Blythe's eyebrows rose. That didn't sound like the man she'd gotten to know when they were all living on the streets.

"I know, I know, I always said I was too proud to accept help. But I was wrong. Refusing help was hurting my Louise, and I was too stubborn to admit that I needed help too. These are good people," he told her. "Let them help. You can repay their kindness when you're back on your feet again."

Feeling weak and overwhelmed, Blythe leaned into Sawyer's hand and sighed in relief when she felt him move behind her so she was practically giving him all her weight. His hand shifted to rest low on her hip, and she could feel his warmth from her thighs to her upper back. All she could do was nod at her old friend.

"Thank you for calling everyone," Sawyer told

Sophie. "And thank you all for coming. Give Blythe a day or two to settle in before you all descend on her like a pack of locusts, all right?"

Everyone chuckled but agreed.

"You ready to go?" he asked, leaning down. And once more, Blythe felt his breath on the side of her neck.

She nodded.

The people parted as if by magic and Squirrel escorted her through all of his friends toward the front door.

"I ordered a bunch of stuff," Beth called after them. "Overnight. Most of it should start arriving later today or tomorrow."

Squirrel lifted his hand in thanks but didn't stop his movement toward the door.

Just as they got there, and the doors opened, Sledge said, "Welcome to our family, Blythe."

The hospital doors closed behind them and Blythe looked up at Sawyer. "What just happened?"

He grinned, the sight making her knees weak. "You just met your new brothers, sisters, aunts, uncles, and cousins, so to speak. We're a large weird family, one that's not connected by blood, but by the bonds of friendship."

For someone who hadn't cried since her mom had passed away, Blythe was finding herself doing it a lot lately. She didn't answer but allowed Sawyer to lead her to a Jeep Wrangler. He helped her in, buckled her seatbelt for her, then went around to the driver's side.

Without a word, he started the engine and pulled out of the parking spot.

Blythe did her best to stay awake, but within minutes she was dead to the world.

CHAPTER SIX

Squirrel pulled into the driveway at Sophie's old house and cut the engine. He sat there for a long moment, simply watching Blythe sleep. She was a mess. Dirty, and he could still see a smear of blood on her neck. Her clothes were tattered and torn, and the smell emanating from her hadn't lessened much with her stay in the hospital.

But it all didn't matter. The outer trappings didn't concern him. Who she was as a person did. He could've sat there all day watching her sleep, but he wanted to get her inside and settled more than he wanted to satisfy his own wants and needs.

He eased his door open and grabbed the bag of meds he'd stopped to pick up on the way home and her backpack. Shrugging it onto his back, he walked around his Jeep and opened her door. Blythe's head was bent at an awkward angle and she seemed to be fast asleep. He unbuckled her seat belt and scooped her up into his arms.

She woke up enough to mumble, "My bag?"

"I've got it, baby. Relax."

"Mmmkay."

Squirrel shut the door with a foot and headed for the house. Sophie had told him earlier that she'd left the front door unlocked when she'd left for the hospital, making their entrance easy. He strode toward the back hallway once they were inside.

He went straight into the master bedroom and to the attached bath. He settled Blythe on the counter and held her upright as he woke her.

"Blythe? Wake up, baby. We're home."

It took her a moment, but finally her eyes opened all the way and she stared at him.

"We are?"

"Yeah."

"I didn't mean to fall asleep."

"It's okay. I bet you haven't had a good night's sleep in a long time."

"You'd win that bet," she told him.

"I would've let you sleep, but I'm guessing you want to shower."

"Oh, God, yes."

"I need to get a plastic bag for your hand and also cover those other wounds before you get in though."

"I can do it," she told him.

"I know. But today you don't have to. Let me help you." Squirrel saw her hesitation. "I already saw them when the doctor stitched you up, remember? Besides, I'm a paramedic. I've seen more naked torsos than the most successful porn star."

She smiled at that.

Pressing his advantage and not giving her a chance to come up with an excuse for him not to help, Squirrel ordered, "Stay there. I'll be right back." He removed her backpack and placed it on the floor next to the counter she was sitting on, then hurried out of the room.

It took him longer than he would've liked to find the plastic wrap and tape, but when he got back to the bathroom, Blythe was still sitting right where he'd left her. She'd kicked off her shoes, and seeing her sitting there, vulnerable and uneasy in her socks, hit him hard.

He helped her stand, making sure she was steady before he let go. Then, trying to ignore anything but the task at hand, he got to work taping the plastic wrap over her stitches. When he was done, he made the mistake of looking at Blythe's face.

Her eyes were closed, and she was clinging to the counter behind her as if her life depended on it.

He didn't see pain in her expression but had to ask. "Did I hurt you?"

"No," she answered immediately.

Squirrel took hold of her uninjured hand clutching the edge of the counter. "Are you sure? It's okay to be in pain. I'm not going to think less of you."

"It's been so long since anyone's touched me," she whispered, her voice breaking. "I can't remember how long. Your fingers on me..." Her eyes opened and she pinned him with her gaze. "They make me feel human for the first time in a really long time."

"Oh, baby..." And with that, Squirrel folded her carefully into his embrace.

What she didn't know was that she made him feel like a man, a true man, for the first time in a really long time too.

He'd always thought of himself as an outsider, awkward. He'd loved school, which wasn't exactly cool, and he had fit in with neither the scholarly crowd nor the athletes. But caring for Blythe, being there for her, made him feel ten feet tall—and suddenly all the labels he'd tried to fit himself into his entire life didn't matter anymore.

He realized that it wasn't looks, or what he wore

or didn't wear, that made someone a man. It was being there for the loved ones in your life. It was letting them cry on you and not feeling awkward about it. It was about doing what was necessary and right, even if it meant they would be upset with you. It was about caring for the people you loved with no expectation of getting anything in return.

The revelation was startling, but the knowledge began to settle deep in his soul. He was beginning to understand...maybe it didn't matter if he wore glasses or wasn't as buff as his friends. Maybe what mattered most was making sure the people he loved were safe.

He set Blythe away from him and reached for the plastic bag. He put it over her injured hand and gently taped it closed around her small wrist. He turned and reached into the shower and turned on the water, testing it until it was the perfect temperature. Hot, but not scalding.

"Be careful with your hand. You're going to have to wash with only the other one, but you can stay in there as long as you want. There's shampoo and conditioner and about four bottles of liquid soap. Apparently, Louise was addicted to the stuff. You have your choice of flowers, flowers, flowers, or gingerbread," he teased. "Take your time, baby. Your stuff is here on the floor; it's safe. I'll close the door and will be in the other room, making you a snack. No one will bother you. Promise."

"Thanks," she told him, biting her lip.

"I know it's morning, but you have to be exhausted. How about if, after your shower, you eat some breakfast then sleep?"

"Okay. But, Sawyer?"

He loved the sound of his name on her lips. "Yeah, baby?"

"You don't have to babysit me. I know you have things to do."

He shook his head. "Nope. You heard Sledge say that the chief gave me some time off."

"But you can't just sit in this house and hover."

"Watch me."

Blythe rolled her eyes. "You're gonna be bored."

"Not a chance in hell. Now hush and shower."

She shook her head but then smiled. "Fine. Out."

Squirrel loved seeing a bit of spunk in her. He'd caught glimpses of it during their conversations but seeing it firsthand was heady. "Yes, ma'am."

He was at the door but turned back. "There're a couple of new toothbrushes under the sink. Help yourself."

Shutting the door behind him, Squirrel went straight to the dresser and pulled open the drawers, looking for something for Blythe to wear. Frustrated when he realized they were all empty, he ran a hand through his hair. He wanted to bring her to his own house but knew that wouldn't go over well. It was a miracle as it was that he got Blythe to agree to come here. All it would take was one wrong move on his part and she'd probably disappear on him.

Remembering the go-bag he had in his Jeep, he spun and left the room. He came back minutes later with one of his Station 7 T-shirts. He kept a couple spare shirts and jeans in his Jeep in case he needed them at work. There had been more than one call when he'd arrived back at the station drenched with sweat. Having a change of clothes handy had become second nature.

He knocked on the bathroom door lightly and when Blythe didn't answer, he cautiously opened it and peeked in. The room was full of steam from the hot shower and he could barely see.

But barely seeing didn't mean *not* seeing. The opaque door to the shower kept him from making out Blythe's form clearly, but what he could see, he liked. She was flushed from the warm water, and her skin contrasted with the white tiles behind her. He watched for a second as she bent back, rinsing her hair, and caught the moan before it left his throat.

The outline of her body, of her tits as she bent backward, made his dick instantly hard.

He turned away, ashamed of himself for looking at Blythe when she was vulnerable. He placed the folded shirt on the counter and eased the door shut. He left the bedroom and entered the kitchen, trying to get himself under control.

Half an hour later, Squirrel heard something behind him and turned.

Blythe slowly walked into the small living room off the kitchen. She was wearing his shirt, which hit her about mid-thigh. She fingered the hem nervously as she stopped and stared at him.

"Hey," she said softly.

"Hey," Squirrel replied. "Shower okay?"

"God, yes," Blythe sighed. "I forgot what a luxury it was to be able to take my time and not have to worry about anyone…er… Anyway, yes, it was nice."

Squirrel felt his muscles tensing at what she didn't say. He took a deep breath to try to calm himself down. "How's your hand?"

She shrugged. "It's okay."

He studied her. She shifted uneasily on her feet and wouldn't meet his gaze. Her brow was furrowed and he didn't miss the way she gingerly held her injured hand in front of her.

"Come sit," he ordered, pulling out a chair at the small table in the kitchen.

She obeyed without question, further telling him

that she wasn't feeling her best. When she got close, he could smell the plumeria soap she'd used in the shower. It fit her. Her cheeks were still flushed from the heat of the water and her skin glowed now that she'd been able to properly clean herself. Squirrel tried not to look at her legs, but he couldn't help it. She had long, slender legs, and when she sat, the hem of his shirt rose up several inches.

A sudden vision of her straddling his lap in a chair just like the one she was sitting in flashed through his brain. His shirt would rise up, and she wouldn't be wearing panties. He'd be able to unzip his jeans, take out his dick, and—

Squirrel shook his head. God, he was an asshole. Blythe was hurt, and probably scared. He shouldn't be thinking about how good she'd feel as he sank inside her.

"Dammit," he mumbled, turning away and heading for the stove.

"What's wrong?" Blythe asked from her seat.

"Nothing," he said immediately, trying to control himself.

"I'm a big girl," she protested. "Don't treat me like a child. It'll just piss me off. If Sophie changed her mind and doesn't want me here, that's fine; just tell me and I'll go."

Squirrel was on his knees at her side before she'd

finished talking. He put one hand on her knee and the other on the side of her neck. "Nothing's wrong. I swear. Sophie wants you here. I was just…" He took a deep breath before continuing, then laid it all on the line. "I'm attracted to you, Blythe. I know you're hungry and I need to feed you. I can tell you're in pain and that you need rest. But seeing you in my shirt, and your bare legs…it's all I can do not to scoop you up and carry you to bed. *That's* why I swore, because you're almost impossible to resist, and the last thing you need right now is to have to fend off a horny male."

She stared down at him in surprise. Her mouth open, eyes wide.

Squirrel moved his hand to the top of her head and ran it over her now clean short hair. He continued his gentle exploration, running his hand over her shoulder then down her arm. He took hold of both wrists gently and held them in her lap. "Can you forgive me for being a letch?"

She smiled then. A grin so big it completely lit up her face. Her gaze dropped and wandered down his body. Squirrel forced himself to remain still, to let her look her fill. He knew with the way he was kneeling next to her there was no way she'd be able to miss his erection, so he didn't try to hide it.

It was obvious when she noticed how hard he

was by her quick inhalation of breath, but she didn't yank out of his grasp. He patiently waited until she was looking him in the eye once again. Her face had a deeper hue of pink from her blush—and it only made him want her all the more.

"I...I don't know what to say."

"You don't have to say anything," he reassured her. "You have nothing to worry about with me. You're safe here. From me, from those assholes who tried to hurt you, and from anything that might try to bring you down. This is your safe haven. A place to regroup and jump-start your life. Got it?"

Blythe bit her lip and didn't look reassured in the least. Squirrel sighed and moved to stand and give her some space.

He didn't get far as her good hand shot out and grabbed his forearm.

"It's been a long time since I've even *thought* about sex. It's hard to think about that when you're hungry, cold, and trying to find a safe place to close your eyes for an hour or so."

Squirrel winced, but she continued.

"It's weird for me to go from thinking I was going to be raped and murdered, to being surrounded by people who say they only want to help me. Even weirder to be sitting here in front of the man who has literally been my lifeline for months, and to realize that my libido picked a hell of a time to kick back in. I...I think I want you too, Squirrel. But I'm not ready."

"Then we'll wait. We'll wait until you're sure you want me, baby. There's no rush. I'm an ass for even bringing it up. You've got enough on your plate right now."

She squeezed his arm. "Don't apologize for being honest, for not hiding your feelings for me. On the streets, people would lie to their mothers if it got them something they wanted or needed."

"I won't ever lie to you, Blythe. Swear."

As if his words were exactly what she needed to hear, Squirrel could practically see the muscles in her body relax.

"I'm gonna make you an omelet. Is that all right?"

"I haven't had eggs in forever. Real eggs, that is. Not the boxed stuff they serve at the shelters."

"Good. There's not much in the way of fillings, but I found some cheese and some red and green peppers that are still edible. That work?"

"Sounds heavenly," Blythe replied. Her eyes darted down once more to between his thighs, then skittered away. "Are you...does that hurt?"

Squirrel stood and leaned over. He kissed the top of her head then put a finger under her chin and gently encouraged her to look at him. "Don't worry about me. I'll take care of it after you fall asleep and I'm in the shower."

She gaped at him. "I can't believe you just said that!"

"What? That I'm going to masturbate?"

She closed her eyes. "Stop. This is so embarrassing."

Squirrel grinned. She was so much fun to tease. He waited until her eyes opened and she looked at him again. "It's not embarrassing. Since we just said we wouldn't lie to each other, I'll admit that it won't be the first time I've gotten off while thinking about you."

And with that, he caressed the side of her face in a feather-light touch, then turned and went to the stove to make her breakfast.

Blythe knew she was blushing but couldn't help it. She couldn't believe Sawyer had just flat-out admitted that he'd jerked off to thoughts of her. That he was going to do it in the shower after breakfast.

She hadn't lied to him, it'd been forever since she'd had any sexual thoughts whatsoever. Being homeless didn't exactly lend itself to feeling sexy or wanting to hop in bed with someone.

But since she didn't have any clean panties to put on after her shower, she was wearing his shirt, and *only* his shirt. She was particularly in tune with her naked body at the moment because of her attire, and she was damp between her legs—and it wasn't because she hadn't dried off properly after reluctantly stepping out of the heavenly shower.

It wasn't normal to have feelings toward someone so quickly…was it?

She thought about that seriously for a moment. Then had to acknowledge that she'd had feelings for Sawyer way before now. Even though they'd only seen each other that one time, talking to him for months without the complications of sexual attraction had helped her really get to know him.

And since she was trying to be honest with herself, she admitted that she'd already come to rely on him way more than was probably healthy for someone in her situation. But her situation had now changed. She wasn't on the streets anymore, even though she could be back there in a heartbeat.

She liked Sawyer. Liked him a lot. And if pressed, she knew she'd probably say yes to anything he wanted to do with her. That should've scared her, but it didn't. Because she knew the kind of man Sawyer was.

Good.   Honest.   Hard-working.   Protective. Generous.

She could go on and on.

She was startled out of her thoughts when Sawyer placed a plate in front of her. Blythe gaped at it. He'd made her the biggest omelet she'd ever seen. He'd also melted cheese inside the eggs but garnished it with more on top as well.

"I can't eat all that!" she exclaimed.

Sawyer merely shrugged. "Then eat as much as you can. I'll put the rest away and you can have it when you get up later."

"Thank you."

"You never have to thank me for feeding you, baby."

Blythe looked up in surprise at the seriousness of his words. He was staring down at her with a look she couldn't decipher.

"It kills me knowing that you're so slender because you weren't getting enough to eat. I hate that you were forced to rely on the charity of those shelters for food. And I'm not an idiot…I know that when you couldn't get into one, you either went hungry or scavenged what you could. The last thing you ever have to worry about again is finding some-thing to eat. You want doughnuts? I'll run out and get them for you. Have a craving for sushi? No problem, I'll make that happen. Making you an omelet for breakfast is my pleasure, Blythe."

"I don't want to always be in your debt. I don't want you to look at me and only see the homeless woman I was. If you can't get past it, whatever this is between us will never work out." She was scared to say the words, but she had to.

Squirrel pulled out a chair next to her and settled in. He leaned toward her on his elbows and said, "When I look at you, I see an amazing woman who's overcome incredible odds. I've put labels on people my entire life, myself included, and you've helped me realize that's not a good way to live, nor is it fair. The fact that you were homeless is not who you are. It's what *happened* to you. There's a difference."

"If you're always going to be worried about whether or not I'm eating, there's no difference."

"Bullshit," he said softly, with no heat behind the word. "I'm always going to be worried about you. That's a guarantee. It makes no difference whether you live in a box on the street or in the world's biggest mansion. Just as I will always worry about my sisters and parents. I want to make sure they're safe, they're happy, and that they have everything they need to be healthy. It's what I do. It's who I am."

"I need to do this by myself," Blythe protested. Not really sure what "this" was, but knowing she needed to somehow find the woman she used to be before she jumped into any kind of relationship where she allowed someone to take care of her.

"You *are* doing this yourself," Sawyer countered. "Accepting help to get back on your feet doesn't mean that you aren't. You're the one who will have to figure out what you want to do for a living, what kind of apartment you can afford, where you want to go from here. But I hope like hell you'll let me stand by your side as you figure it all out."

Blythe couldn't help but grin. "Stand by my side holding a hotdog and feeding it to me when I'm hungry, right?"

He returned her smile. "Exactly. Now eat before it gets cold."

She rolled her eyes but picked up her fork and dug in. After a few bites, she asked, "Aren't you having anything?"

Sawyer shook his head. "Nope. I'll grab something later."

She should've felt self-conscious eating in front of him, but the eggs were so good and he kept up an easy, light conversation. By the time she realized she was full, she'd eaten over half the omelet.

She sat back in the chair and patted her belly. "I'm done."

"You did good," Sawyer commented. "Ate more

than I thought you would." He stood and grabbed her plate. He went to the counter and she watched from the table as he covered the rest of the omelet and put it in the fridge. Then he poured a large glass of water and shook a pill into his palm from a bottle on the counter.

He brought both back to the table. "I'm sorry there's nothing but water for now. Driftwood and Taco will get whatever you want from the store later today."

"It's fine," Blythe told him and downed the pill he handed her without even asking what it was. She hoped it was a painkiller, as whatever the doctor had used to numb her wounds was wearing off.

"Come on, let's get you settled."

Blythe put her hand in his and let him pull her upright. He turned and led her back down the hallway to the master bedroom. "Need to use the restroom before you lay down?"

She shook her head.

He pulled back the covers and motioned for her to crawl in. Blythe did as directed, then sighed in contentment at the smell of the clean sheets, the soft, non-lumpy mattress under her, and the nice plump pillow beneath her head.

"Comfy?" Sawyer asked with an amused smile on his face.

"Very."

Blythe's eyes widened slightly as he leaned over her. She thought he was going to kiss her on the forehead, but instead, his lips brushed against her own. He hesitated a fraction of a second, then increased the pressure. She felt his tongue lick against her lower lip, but before she could do more than breathe in through her nose, he'd pulled back.

His eyes were heavy-lidded and she saw his nostrils flare before he said, "Sleep well, baby. I'll be nearby if you want anything."

Blythe looked around the room, searching for her bag.

"What are you looking for?" Sawyer asked.

She hated to be needy, but she'd guarded the phone he'd accidentally given her for so long, she wasn't sure she could sleep without it now. "My bag."

"It's in the bathroom still. What do you need?"

"The phone?" It came out as a question, which Blythe hated, but Sawyer didn't seem to notice. He immediately spun on his heels and disappeared into the bathroom. He returned with her pack. He put it on the floor next to the bed and raised his eyebrows, as if to ask if it was okay for him to look inside.

Blythe nodded and he quickly pulled out his old cell phone. He handed it to her without a word.

"Thanks."

"You're welcome. Try to get some sleep," he ordered.

"Good night," Blythe told him.

Sawyer nodded at her, then turned and left the room.

Blythe clutched the phone to her chest for a long moment after he left, then took a deep breath and turned it on.

It immediately began to vibrate with incoming messages.

Natalie: OMG. U ok? Txt wen u can.

Charlotte: Heard you were hurt. That sucks. Text later so I can show you my dress for the dance.

Emma: Mom said something happened. I hope you're okay. If you need anything, just ask! We wanted to come but Sawyer said we had to wait.

Blythe couldn't help but chuckle. Sawyer's sisters were so different, but each showed their concern in their own way.

Seeing such worry from his family made her think of Hope and Billy once more. Where were they right now? Who was worrying about *them*...well, besides her? The thought made her sad and anxious.

Without thinking about what she was doing, she clicked on Squirrel's name and sent a text.

Blythe: You have an amazing family.

She didn't have to wait more than a few seconds for him to respond.

Squirrel: They're a pain in the ass, but I couldn't love them more. You okay?

Blythe: Yeah. I'm just used to texting you right before I go to sleep.

Squirrel: You can text me any time, any place. But you know all you need to do is call out and I'll be in there in two seconds, right?

Blythe: I know.

Blythe: Sawyer?

Squirrel: Yeah, baby?

Blythe: Thank you.

Squirrel: You're welcome. Now go to sleep. I need to shower. ;)

*Blythe: *eye roll* Stop talking about that.*

Squirrel: What? I'm dirty. I need to get clean.

Blythe: When did our texting cross the line into sexual innuendos?

Squirrel: The second I saw you in that hospital bed and decided I wasn't going to let you go. Sleep, woman.

Blythe's stomach clenched at his reply, but the smile didn't leave her face.

Blythe: Bossy.

Squirrel: Yup. You aren't sleeping.

Blythe: Zzzzzzzzzz

She clicked off the phone out of habit after she hit send. The battery was getting low, and she also didn't want it vibrating while she was sleeping in case someone heard it and decided they wanted to steal—

Blythe blinked when she realized she didn't need to worry about someone stealing her phone, or anything else while she was sleeping.

Because she was safe. In a house. With Sawyer in the other room.

Within moments, she was asleep.

* * *

After a shower, Squirrel slowly pushed open the door to the bedroom and saw Blythe asleep on the bed. He quietly walked over to her side and stood there, staring down at her. He wanted to touch her. Wanted to pull her into his arms and reassure her that she was safe, but he didn't.

She needed time and he was going to give it to her, no matter how much it pained him.

As he'd sat in the other room, with only a wall separating them, texting her because it was her nighttime ritual, Squirrel came to the realization that he'd do anything for Blythe.

He'd scrolled through their text conversations from the past…and it hit him.

He admired her. Liked her. She was thoughtful, funny, smart.

And he loved her.

She wouldn't believe him. Hell, his own friends would probably tell him he was crazy. That there was no way he could love a woman he'd seen a grand total of two times in his life. But he knew it was true. She'd reached down inside his chest and grabbed hold of his heart and wouldn't let go.

He didn't want her to let go.

Vowing to keep his newly discovered feelings to

himself for as long as it took Blythe to get her life back on track, Squirrel took a deep breath and slowly, quietly backed out of the room.

He'd wait. As long as it took. But no way in hell was he leaving her alone. She'd have to get used to seeing him. Every time she turned around, he'd be there. Supporting her, cheering her on, loving her.

When the door snicked shut, Blythe's eyes opened and she stared at where she knew Sawyer had been standing. What had he seen when he'd looked at her? What had he been thinking?

Blythe had woken the moment he'd opened the door. Living on the streets had made her hyper-aware to even the slightest sound. He'd showered, as he said he would. She could smell the clean, fresh scent of soap lingering in his wake. And all Blythe could think of was what he'd said he was going to do. Had he? Had he stroked himself thinking about her until he'd orgasmed?

The thought had her shifting on the bed. She was wet between her thighs again. And it felt so different, vulnerable, sleeping almost nude. Since she'd been living on the streets, she'd been sleeping in all of her clothes, just in case.

Blythe's hand slipped down her body tentatively. Did she even remember how to get herself off? What if she couldn't do it anymore?

Her index finger touched her clit and she jolted, then bit back a moan.

As she reacquainted herself with her own body, Blythe thought about Sawyer. She remembered all of his words of support and the way he'd begged her to let him help her.

Her thoughts turned to how she'd felt when he'd stood behind her in the hospital, how big and strong he'd felt at her back.

Her fingers moved faster and faster between her legs, the pleasure rising like a tidal wave. She couldn't remember ever coming this fast, but it had been a really long time since she'd felt any desire at all; she figured she was overdue.

Sighing in contentment after she'd come, Blythe gingerly turned onto her side, not even caring that it put pressure on one of her knife wounds. She was in an unfamiliar bed, it was dark, she was exhausted and in pain...but none of that seemed to matter. Not with Sawyer being just one yell away.

CHAPTER SEVEN

A week later, on the first night Sawyer had to be back at work, Blythe was sitting at the small kitchen table examining the classified ads in the paper. She needed to get a job but couldn't seem to find anything that appealed. At least nothing she was qualified for. Then there was the matter of not having a car, of needing to open a bank account... but she had no *money* to open an account.

Everything seemed so complicated, but she was sick of being homeless. Of having to accept charity from her new friends. She wanted a job. Wanted to support herself again.

Sawyer had wanted to help her look for employment, but she hadn't felt brave enough to tell him her entire story yet. She just wasn't ready to talk about all the circumstances that had led her to being homeless. She was embarrassed, even if he told her time and time again that ending up on the streets was nothing to be ashamed about.

She'd get there. Blythe knew she'd eventually tell Sawyer everything. Every day she spent with him made her surer of that, but for now, he was giving her space and letting her try to figure things out on her own, which she appreciated.

What she wasn't so sure about was sleeping in the house by herself. It was silly, really. But she hadn't been alone in so long, it felt really weird to be so now. On the streets, there were always people around. In the sleeping room at the shelter, walking around, even sleeping under trash bins or in the park. Someone was *always* there.

Over the last week, Sawyer had spent as much time as possible with her, keeping his word to do what he could to make sure she wasn't alone. They'd spent many evenings just chatting about nothing in particular. They'd played a few board games and watched TV together. One afternoon, they'd sat in silence while each was reading a book. She had a copy of a romance one of the other women had brought over and he was reading a western. It had been comfortable and so darn normal.

Even the other women had visited when Sawyer had been running errands. Adeline had come over with Coco, her service dog, and Blythe hadn't laughed like she had with her in a long time. They'd tried to make some complicated meal for Sawyer when he got back, but it had failed miserably. Sophie had shown up another afternoon and they'd passed the time talking about what it was like dating a firefighter and Sophie told her as much as she could about Roman's Native American heritage and all about the ceremony they'd participated in after the huge fire next to the hospital she worked at.

Driftwood and Taco had gone to the store and arrived with enough food to feed an army that first night and Sawyer made all of her favorite dishes... after he'd threatened to make her tofu or liver and onions if she didn't tell him what she missed eating the most.

But now, for the first time since getting off the streets, she was utterly alone. Blythe had tried to turn on the radio to fill the empty space with music, but it had creeped her out because she couldn't hear if someone was breaking into the house or sneaking up on her. It was ridiculous, because it wasn't like Sophie's house was in a crime-ridden area or anything, but old habits were hard to break.

The clothes Beth had ordered arrived the day after she'd gotten there. She'd gone way overboard, and Blythe had told Sawyer she was going to return most of them. He'd apparently tattled on her, and Beth had called about an hour later and told her that if she returned anything for any reason other than fit, Beth would only order *more* clothes.

In order to prevent the woman from buying out Macy's, Blythe had acquiesced.

The wounds on her sides were healing nicely and didn't hurt anymore. Her hand was still giving her problems, but Sawyer had been unwrapping it and treating it every night. Making sure it wasn't infected and keeping his eye on the stitches. He'd explained that it would heal slower because of where the cut was and because it was a deeper wound. Blythe couldn't deny the small thrill that shot through her body when he gently kissed the skin around the cut before wrapping it back up each night.

She could tell Sawyer was trying hard not to be bossy, but he still was. He forced her to take walks with him to get some fresh air when all she wanted to do was hide inside. He made her eat not only three meals a day, but small snacks in between as well. He researched the best foods for gaining weight in a healthy way and followed the recommendations of the experts to a tee.

But for some reason, his bossiness didn't bother her. He wasn't a dick about it, but he also wouldn't budge when she protested. Deep down, Blythe knew why she wasn't bothered by his persistence. First, it had been a long time since anyone had cared enough about her to make sure she ate healthy, got enough sleep, and wasn't hurting. Second…he was becoming even more important to her. She liked him, a lot.

He had his quirks. He was a little too obsessed with the murder channel on television, was too quick with the self-deprecating jokes when he was around his friends, and he seemed to put others first too often. But none of those things were actually turnoffs.

The dichotomy that was Sawyer McClay was interesting. He was a firefighter and a paramedic, so he was brave and had no trouble rushing into burning buildings or climbing under a wrecked car to get to someone who was injured. But he seemed to have doubts about his own good looks and desirability to women.

Blythe could have assured him that he shouldn't have any worries in that arena. But she could tell he was self-conscious about his glasses, and the fact he wasn't as muscular as his friends. He'd made fun of himself more than once when Sophie and Chief had come over. Saying that he was Clark Kent while his friends were more like Superman.

It bothered Blythe, and she wanted to make him see himself as *she* saw him. As a hero. *Her* hero.

A loud knock on the door brought Blythe out of her musings and scared the shit out of her. Who in the world could be at the door? It was eight-thirty at night. Sawyer was at the station on his shift. And she didn't know anyone else.

Walking silently on bare feet to the door, Blythe peeked out of the peephole and gasped in surprise. Moving quickly, she unlocked the bolt and opened the door.

Standing on the front porch was Sophie, Adeline and her dog, Beth and *her* dog, Quinn, and Penelope.

And the weirdest thing about the group wasn't that they were here at all, but the tiny donkey that was standing next to Penelope.

"Hello," Blythe said tentatively.

"Hi!" Adeline chirped happily. "We're here for a girls-night-in party."

"Um…" Blythe said, completely confused.

"Squirrel said it was your first night alone in the house, and he didn't like that," Penelope told her. "He arranged for us to come over and have a slumber party so you didn't have to be alone."

"I have to be alone at some point," Blythe responded reasonably.

"Lucky for you, that's not tonight. Now move, so we can come inside with all our shit," Beth said.

Blythe loved how blunt the other woman was. She stepped back and watched as everyone came inside the small house with their bags. It took Adeline and Penelope an extra trip back to the car to get all of the things for their animals as well.

The living room was stuffed full of people and animals by the time everyone got settled. Quinn was in the kitchen pouring drinks with Sophie, and that left Blythe with Adeline, Beth, Penelope, and their pets. "So..." She gestured to the dogs and donkey.

"Coco is my service dog. He detects seizures," Adeline explained.

"You're epileptic?" Blythe asked tentatively.

She nodded. "Yup. Although I had brain surgery not too long ago, and the number of seizures I have was reduced almost ninety percent. I still get them now and then, but nowhere like the two or three I was having a day."

"Wow. How does he know?"

Adeline shrugged. "No clue. But he always seems to sense when one's coming on. He gives me enough time to get somewhere safe where I won't get hurt when I seize."

"Cool. And *your* dog?" Blythe asked Beth. The

other woman was sitting in a corner of the couch, her dog lying next to her, his head in her lap.

"His name is Second. Like, for second chance. Both for him and me. One of our other friends, Laine, found his mom and brothers and sisters at an old farm that was for sale. His mom saved Laine, and she saved them in return. I have agoraphobia, PTSD, and anxiety. He helps me to not be such a freak when I leave the house." Beth petted Second's head lovingly.

"I'm sorry," Blythe said softly.

Beth shrugged. "Don't be. I'm good. I'm sure you'll hear my story eventually, but basically, I'm very lucky to be alive. I can deal with all the other shit because of that fact."

Blythe moved so she could reach the other woman and put her hand over her foot. "Are you okay?"

Beth smiled at her. "Yeah. After...what I'd been through, I thought my life was ruined forever. And I did look at it that way, for a really long time. But then I met Cade and realized that my life is what I make of it. I could live in the past and be bitter and angry forever, but what would that get me? So, with Second's help, I'm trying to live every day like it's the best day of my life."

Blythe gaped at Beth. She hadn't pegged her for

being the philosophical type. But then again, she didn't know exactly what had happened to her. And the more she thought about it, the more she liked Beth's outlook on life.

"And this is Smokey," Penelope said, breaking the silence. "He's my service donkey."

Everyone giggled. Sophie and Quinn came back into the room just then and handed out green drinks to everyone.

"What the hell is this?" Beth asked, staring at the drink skeptically.

"It's called an alien s-secretion," Sophie informed them.

"Do we want to know what's in it?" Blythe asked. She couldn't remember the last time she'd had a drink. Hell, the last time she'd sat around not worrying about money, her mom, where she was going to get a meal, or where she was going to sleep.

Suddenly, she didn't give one shit about what was in the drink she was about to consume. She was just happy to be hanging out with women she genuinely liked.

"Coconut rum, m-melon liqueur, vodka, and pineapple juice."

Blythe took a sip—and coughed. "Good God, you're trying to kill us. Did you use any juice in here at all?"

Everyone chuckled and, surprisingly, Smokey brayed, throwing his head up and down as if he too wanted to join in the fun.

That set them all off even more, and before long, all six women were laughing their heads off. When everyone had settled down, Penelope explained how she came to have a service donkey.

"I found him in the middle of a forest fire. He was basically on fire and came to us for help. I doused his body and he followed us. Refused to go back to wherever he came from." She shrugged. "So, I took him home."

"Tell her why he's good for you," Beth encouraged.

The petite woman smoothed a lock of blonde hair behind her ear, looking anywhere but at the women around her, then concentrated on petting the donkey's head in her lap. Finally, she sighed and said softly, "When I was in the Army, I was kidnapped overseas by terrorists. They held me for quite a while...always threatening to kill me. Killing other soldiers right in front of me. I was rescued, but I... It's hard to deal with some days."

Blythe could sympathize. She hadn't been kidnapped by terrorists, but she knew how hard it could be to deal with your past. And now that she thought about it, she remembered all the news stories about the "American Princess." Her mom had still been alive then, and they'd had a conversation one night after Penelope was rescued about how the poor woman was going to have to have a lot of therapy to get through what had happened to her.

"Smokey doesn't care that I need to keep the light on to sleep. He doesn't care that I feel completely screwed up in the head. He doesn't boss me around, he's simply glad to see me every time I visit him."

"Does he stay in your house?" Blythe asked.

Penelope pouted. "No. My landlord would have a shit fit. Right now, Moose is keeping him for me."

"Moose. He's one of the other firefighters, right?" Blythe asked.

"Yeah. A bossy, overbearing, pain-in-the-ass firefighter," Penelope returned. She took a large swig of her drink, then added quietly, "And one I love so much, sometimes it hurts to be around him."

Blythe blinked.

"It's about time you admitted it," Beth said.

"It's not like we all didn't already know how you felt about him," Sophie added.

"He's crazy about you too," Adeline added.

"I'm confused," Quinn said.

Blythe was glad she said it, because she was lost too.

"If you love him, and he loves you back, why aren't you with him?" Quinn asked.

"Because!" Penelope practically shouted. "I'm a mess! And we're total opposites. He's amazing and so put together it makes me feel bad simply being around him. I know he just feels responsible for me. If he got to know me, *really* know me, see what was in my head, he'd run in the opposite direction so fast it would make my head spin."

"You know that's not true," Adeline said softly.

"It is. I'm doing what's best for him."

"But what about what's best for you?" Beth asked. "I mean, love conquers all, and all that shit."

Quinn sighed. "You guys crack me up, and not always in a good way."

Everyone's eyes swung to her, and Blythe could see her swallow hard before speaking.

"I mean, look at all of you. You've all got men who would move heaven and earth for you. Do you know how rare and awesome that is? Soph, your man went into a burning building, even though it definitely wasn't safe, to find you. Adeline, I heard Dean almost killed the guy who broke into your hotel room. Beth, it's more than obvious how far Cade would go for you. Even when he knew you were struggling with pyromania, he didn't give up on you. Blythe, Squirrel asked all of us to come over tonight and make sure you were good to go on your first night alone. And, Penelope, I can't believe you're hesitating for one second to grab that huge hunk of a man who is keeping your *donkey* at his house, for God's sake. You're insane. Seriously.

"The problem is, none of you have ever known what it's like to not be wanted. All my life, I've been shunned because of this stupid mark on my face. Did I ask for it? No. Did I deserve for my birth mother to refuse to touch me because she thought I'd been marked by the devil? No. Did I deserve to be shuttled from one foster home to another and for kids to bully me throughout school? *No*. But I understand it. When push comes to shove, you have to love yourself before anyone else can."

Everyone was silent after the somewhat shy woman's outburst.

"Holy s-shit," Sophie muttered. "Quinn's emerged from her s-shell."

"Oh, I have not. I still don't like being the center of attention," she countered. "But I can't stand for Penelope to be so down on herself. You were a soldier. You somehow survived the worst shit that's out there. You not only made it through being kidnapped, you didn't die when that rescue helicopter crashed. And now you have a kick-ass pet, a group of firefighters who would do anything for you, and an alpha male who looks at you with the most pathetic googly eyes I've ever seen on someone his size and with his overload of testosterone. I don't think you have any reason to be hesitant when it comes to Moose. I envy you, Penelope. Hell, I envy *all* of you."

And with that, she drained the rest of her drink with one gulp.

"Anyone want another?" she asked, waiting about two seconds before standing and stomping off into the kitchen to get a refill.

"Well, all right then," Penelope muttered.

"Someone's been gossiping," Beth said with a grin as she stared at Sophie.

"S-She's m-my friend. Of course I'm going to gossip with her," the other woman shrugged.

"She's right," Blythe said. "I mean, we're all really lucky. I feel incredibly blessed to have met all of you and that you're here right now." She looked at Sophie. "You were the first person to make me and Tadd feel like actual human beings out there on the street. You didn't care if we smelled because we hadn't showered or if our clothes were dirty and torn."

"That s-stuff doesn't m-matter," Sophie said softly.

"It does to a lot of people. *Most* people," Blythe

countered. "Tadd and Louise really needed help after they were hurt, and you didn't even hesitate to offer them your house. Heck, I'm sure you didn't when Sawyer asked if I could stay here either, did you?"

"Nope. Not for a s-second," Sophie told her with a grin.

"It's been a long time since I've had friends. Thank you all for coming over. I didn't admit to Sawyer that I was nervous, but he obviously knew anyway."

"Why do you call him Sawyer?" Beth asked.

Blythe shrugged. "He doesn't seem like a 'Squirrel' to me. Why is that his nickname, anyway?"

Penelope raised her hand in the air excitedly, as if she were a first grader in a classroom full of students who knew the answer.

"Why yes, Penelope? You'd like to tell us the answer?" Adeline asked dryly.

She nodded. "Because when he first started at the station, we got a 'cat stuck in a tree' call. While the guys were trying to figure out how to get the ladder truck close enough to the tree and not ruin the landscaping, he just walked over and scampered up it like he climbed trees every day. I think it was Sledge who first said he looked like a squirrel, the way he shimmied up the tree. It stuck."

"He doesn't exactly fit in with the others, does

he?" Quinn asked as she came back into the room with a full drink. "I mean, he kinda reminds me of that Reed guy on *Criminal Minds*."

Blythe's eyes narrowed, and she said with more heat than she intended, "What are you saying? That he's a nerd? That he's not as attractive as the other guys? That's bull. I think his glasses make him look sophisticated. And who cares anyway? Everyone doesn't have to be a cover model."

Quinn sat on the edge of the couch and held up her hands in capitulation. "No, no, no. I didn't mean it in a bad way. Squirrel is hot. Not hot in an '*I* want to do him' way, because I'm not attracted to him. I mean, I would be if I didn't already like Driftwood. He's just not my type but he's good-looking for sure." Quinn's words were rushed and she almost tripped over them, trying to get them out and not offend her new friend.

Blythe stared at Quinn for a moment, then smiled. Then before she knew it, she was laughing so hard she thought she was going to pee her pants. Soon, everyone joined in until the room was filled with laughter.

When Blythe had herself under control, she asked, "So...you and Driftwood?"

Quinn's cheeks turned bright red and she stammered, "Oh...no...I was just—"

"Don't lie," Sophie admonished her. "You like him!"

"Quinn and Driftwood sittin' in a tree, K-I-S-S-I-N-G," Adeline sang.

"Stop it," Quinn ordered, glaring at the other woman.

"It's not a crime to admit that you like him," Beth told her.

Quinn shrugged. "He's…too much for me."

"Didn't you just give us a speech about how, if you had a man like ours, you'd snatch him up and never let go?" Beth countered. "Driftwood *is* a man like ours. And it's obvious he likes you."

"He just feels sorry for me," Quinn said.

Penelope snorted. "Pa-leeze. Girl, you aren't any different from me! You just sat there and gave me a big ol' lecture about how Moose didn't feel responsible for me, when you can't see what's right in front of your face. You insinuated that you've never been wanted before, but what you aren't seeing, or are refusing to acknowledge for some reason, is that there's a man who's trying really hard to show you exactly how much *he* wants you. Driftwood soaks up every scrap of information he can get about you. You should see him grill Chief when he knows he and Soph have hung out with you. And the next time I see Driftwood, he's not going to let me do anything until he hears every little detail about tonight. What you were wearing—cute top, by the way—if you looked okay, if we did anything to make you feel self-conscious. Quinn, the man is into you. *Way* into you. Throw him a bone, would ya?"

Everyone was silent as Quinn digested Penelope's words. "I just...I've been let down so many times, I don't think I have it in me to give anyone a chance to hurt me again."

"A bit ago, you told us that you have to love yourself before anyone else can," Sophie reminded her. "And while I agree with that, I think that in s-some cases, if you allow s-someone else to love you first, that person can help you *learn* to love yourself."

"I hadn't thought about it that way," Quinn said.

"You make a very good point, my friend," Penelope told Sophie.

"What about being friends with him? You can do that, can't you?" Adeline asked.

Quinn sighed. "That's not fair to him. I've been there. Liked a boy so much, only to be disappointed when nothing happened."

"Driftwood is not a boy," Penelope insisted. "He's a man. A good man. I don't know what happened to you in the past, but I can guarantee that Driftwood is nothing like those who have hurt you."

Sophie leaned over and put her hand on her friend's leg in silent support.

"I'll think about it," Quinn finally said.

Smokey surprised everyone by getting up from his place beside Penelope and walking over to Quinn. He put his head in her lap and looked up at her with big brown eyes, as if he understood the pain she was feeling.

"He's quite the empath," Penelope said smugly. "He always seems to know when people are sad or scared. That's why he's so good for me."

Everyone laughed but didn't disagree.

"I'm going to let Coco out. Second, you need to go?" Adeline asked.

As if he understood, the other dog barked once and went right to the door.

"Might as well take Smokey out too," Penelope said.

"He's potty-trained?" Blythe asked in surprise.

"Not really, but I keep hoping."

Everyone chuckled.

Blythe stood and went into the kitchen as the others accompanied their animals outside. Quinn slipped into the bathroom, probably to compose herself. Sophie followed Blythe into the kitchen.

"You doing okay?" Sophie asked.

"Yeah." She turned to the other woman. "I can't

thank you enough for letting me stay here. I'm going to get out of your hair as soon as I can—"

Sophie held up a hand. "S-Stop it. You can s-stay here as long as you want. I'm not using the house, it's not a problem."

"But you could sell it or something. If I wasn't here—"

"No."

Blythe put down the glass she'd been holding and glared at Sophie. "Stop interrupting me."

"Then s-stop s-saying s-stupid s-shit. Hey… look…four S words in a row. Go m-me!"

Blythe had been ready to lay into Sophie. To tell her that she didn't understand what she was feeling, how she didn't want to take charity, but when Sophie made fun of herself, Blythe found herself smiling instead.

Then, inexplicably, tears sprang to her eyes at Sophie's overwhelming kindness. She turned to busy herself with the alcohol and hoped the other woman hadn't seen.

She considered talking to Sophie about her worry for Hope and Billy. She'd understand and probably rally the troops, so to speak, to try to find them, but the last thing she wanted was to put her, or any of her new friends, in danger. She knew without a doubt Sophie, Adeline, and the others would immediately want to head downtown and start looking, especially since there was a child involved.

Dismissing the idea, she concentrated on the bottle of alcohol in front of her.

"Blythe," Sophie said softly, putting her hand on her shoulder.

Crap. She'd seen her tears. Taking a deep breath, Blythe spoke, not turning to face her new friend. "I've been on my own for a long time. I didn't trust anyone. Then Tadd and Louise showed up and basically forced me to hang out with them. I loved them like they were my parents. Then just like that," she snapped her fingers, "they were gone from my life. I just... Tonight has been awesome. I'm not sure how many more people I can lose from my life and keep going."

"You're not going to lose us," Sophie told her with a hint of steel in her tone.

"Shit happens, Sophie. You can't say that for sure."

"I can and I will. Blythe, I don't know what happened to you in the past, but if you disappeared, I'm not the kind of friend who would s-shrug and think, 'Oh, well, I haven't heard from Blythe in a while, s-she m-must not like m-me anymore.' No. If you s-sneak out in the m-middle of the night, I'm going to find you. Unlike S-Squirrel, I'll totally let Beth track your ass down."

Blythe turned to her then. "What do you mean?"

"Beth asked S-Squirrel to let her track you by your phone, but he wouldn't let her. S-Said that you were an adult and that s-she had to treat you like one. But it hurt him, m-make no m-mistake. Penelope s-said s-she could s-see how worried he was about you. Then when you called about M-Milena and her friend being kidnapped by that crazy pedophile guy, he was done. Decided that he wasn't going to 'dick around' anymore. His words, not m-mine. Told Beth to do what s-she could to find you. Chief told m-me he s-spent quite a few of his days off looking for you. But every time he got a location from Beth, you'd m-moved."

"He looked for me?" Blythe asked, completely shocked.

"Yeah. He looked for you. I probably wasn't s-supposed to tell you, but whatever. M-My point is, you've got friends who won't let you disappear from our lives like the people in your past obviously did. We don't care if you go from one of our houses to the next, you won't ever have to s-sleep on the s-streets again. Chief even told m-me he s-spoke to Cade, arranging it s-so if you needed it, you could have one of the beds at the fire s-station. Not that it's even necessary because you're at m-my house and I won't let you leave until you have s-somewhere s-stable to go, but s-still."

Blythe was shocked. Completely gobsmacked. "I don't even know Cade."

"It doesn't m-matter. You're dating S-Squirrel. That's enough for him."

"I'm not dating Sawyer," Blythe denied.

Sophie's eyebrows raised. "Really? S-So him s-sleeping here for the past week didn't m-mean anything? Him asking m-me if you could s-stay here, and insisting on paying the m-mortgage while you're here, doesn't m-mean anything? Him asking Beth to get you s-some clothes, having the guys s-shop and fill the house with food, and him calling all of us and arranging this little s-slumber party doesn't m-mean anything?"

Blythe didn't know what to say. Her chest was tight and she pressed her lips together to try to stem the sobs she knew were only a heartbeat away from escaping.

Sophie's tone gentled. "And what about his family? He knew his s-sisters were texting you, Blythe. There's *no one* he doesn't protect m-more in this life than them. You think if he didn't care about you, that he'd let them think you were his girlfriend? If he was helping you out of pity or s-some other reason, I can tell you he'd never, ever let them be involved with you in any way."

"I'm afraid all this will be taken away, just like everything else good in my life has been."

"Then don't let it," Sophie retorted. "Fight for it. Let us help you. No s-strings attached, Blythe. I promise."

A vision suddenly popped into Blythe's mind. She could see herself sitting in a chair holding an infant, surrounded by a roomful of laughing people. Her friends. Children ran around screaming in joy as they played. Everywhere she looked, she saw smiles and happiness.

Then she felt a hand on her shoulder, and as the man behind her leaned close, Blythe knew it was Sawyer. She recognized him by his scent. His hand caressed her arm as he interlaced his fingers with hers under the baby in her arms. He turned his head, and Blythe shivered as his warm breath wafted over her neck and ear when he whispered, "The happiest day of my life was the day you became my wife, but seeing you sitting here, holding our child, surrounded by the most important people in our lives, just might top it."

She blinked as Sophie brought her out of her vivid daydream by asking, "Blythe? You okay?"

It had seemed so real.

With a pang, Blythe realized she wanted that dream. Wanted that child, that life.

And in order to get it, she had to accept the fact that she needed help. She didn't want to live on the streets for the rest of her life. She wanted Sawyer. And his child. To be in the middle of a large group of friends who treated each other like family.

"I'm not going to disappear," she told Sophie. "I don't know what I'm going to do or how I'm going to get back on my feet, but I promise, I won't run. I don't want to go back to the streets."

A huge smile spread across Sophie's face. "Good. Hurry up and refill those glasses. We have s-some alcohol to drink, and I know for a fact that Beth brought over her copy of *Fifty Shades* for us to watch."

"Oooh. I haven't seen it yet," Blythe said.

"I know s-some people didn't like the book, but I have to s-say, it's worth watching the movie just to look at Jamie Dornan."

Blythe smiled at Sophie. "Sounds good."

"It's not good, it's awesome," Sophie returned. "Now come on, let's go!"

Blythe followed Sophie out of the kitchen, somehow feeling a hundred times lighter than she had earlier that night. For the first time in a long time, she felt at peace. She knew getting her life back on track wouldn't be easy, but with friends like Sophie, Beth, Adeline, Penelope, and Quinn, it would be a hell of a lot easier than without them.

Hours later, after watching *Fifty Shades*—and the sequel—finishing two bottles of vodka, and laughing hard enough for her stomach to hurt, Blythe glanced around the small room and smiled.

Everyone was asleep but her. Beth was using Second's belly as a pillow. Penelope was sleeping on her stomach on the floor and Smokey had his head resting on her legs. Adeline was snoring slightly in the recliner, Coco at her feet. Quinn was lying across the sofa cushions, her feet in Sophie's lap, who was scrunched up at the other end.

Blythe was sitting in an armchair next to the sofa, and across from Adeline and Coco. She gazed at her friends for a while longer, then quietly got up from the chair. She tiptoed as quietly as possible out of the room and down the hall to the master bedroom.

She went straight to her backpack leaning against the wall.

She'd washed her old clothes, putting them right back inside her backpack afterward, needing to be ready to go at a moment's notice, just in case. Now, she unzipped the bag and methodically took out every piece of clothing inside, which wasn't much. One by one, she brought her three shirts to the drawer that held the new shirts Beth had ordered for her. She then did the same with the two pairs of jeans she owned.

She placed her old ratty panties next to the new lacey ones in another drawer, and she put the sports bra she'd worn almost every day on the streets in with the new lingerie as well.

Then she pulled out the only picture she owned of her and her mother, before she'd gotten sick, and placed it on the small side table next to the bed.

She had a few more odds and ends that she unpacked and placed around the bedroom. Then she zipped up the backpack that had once held all her worldly goods and went into the walk-in closet. She couldn't bring herself to throw it away…yet. She put it on one of the shelves in the back of the closet, out of the way, but still accessible if necessary.

Taking a deep breath, she closed the closet door and padded back to the dresser. She took off her clothes, leaving them where they landed on the floor. Pulling on the Station 7 T-shirt Sawyer had given her, she went into the bathroom to brush her teeth and take care of business. Then she crawled under the covers and reached for her phone.

She quickly typed a text to Sawyer, then shut off the phone without waiting for a response.

Closing her eyes, she relaxed. For the first time

since she'd woken up to the sounds of that couple being robbed back in the alley downtown, Blythe realized that some of the worries she'd been carrying around had dissipated.

She fell asleep immediately, another first, without worrying about what might happen to her while she was sleeping.

* * *

Squirrel heard his phone ding with a text and he snatched it off the small table next to the twin-size bed in one of the sleeping rooms at the station. He'd been thinking about Blythe all night, hoping things were going well.

It was from Blythe. And from the looks of it, she'd probably indulged in quite a few of the drinks Penelope said they were going to have. The message was full of typos, but he could read it just fine.

Blythe: Tanks 4 sendig the girls. I had a grt nite. Havnt had froends in long tome. But that dosnt mean i didnt miss u. im not going to run. Beth wont hav 2 trak me. K?

Squirrel closed his eyes in relief. He'd been worried

about Blythe not being able to handle everything that had happened recently. He knew it was hard for her to accept help. He'd arranged for the women to keep her company in the hopes that it would also keep her from sneaking out in the middle of the night.

He knew from having three sisters that friends were important. As much as he wanted to keep Blythe all to himself, that would never work. Women needed women. Friends. He quickly sent her a text back.

Squirrel: I miss you too, baby. You have no idea how much. And that's good about you stickin' around. But you should know, even if you did run, I'd find you. I don't make the same mistake twice, and letting you refuse my help was a huge one that almost got you killed. Sleep well. I'll see you tomorrow afternoon.

She didn't respond, but Squirrel didn't really expect her to. He placed his cell on the table and lay back against the pillows on the bed in contentment. Hopefully, the rest of the shift went by quickly. He wanted to get back to Blythe.

CHAPTER EIGHT

Squirrel wasn't sure exactly what had happened that night he'd asked Sophie and the other women to keep Blythe company, but whatever it was, it had changed her. In a good way.

She seemed more relaxed in the two weeks since the sleepover. Happier. But more than that, she seemed determined to get her life back on track, rather than merely going through the motions, expecting to be kicked out of his life any day.

Neither had discussed the emotionally charged texts they'd sent each other that night, but Squirrel hadn't forgotten. He'd taken a screenshot of them, and every now and then re-read their words. They seemed like promises. From her that she wouldn't run, and from him that if she did, he'd move heaven and earth to find her.

Squirrel had also made the difficult decision to go back to his house. He really wanted to continue sleeping on the couch at Sophie's house, so he could be close to Blythe, but they were both adults, and if he wanted to get their relationship on an even keel, he had to let her live her life.

That didn't mean it didn't suck.

They still texted a lot, though. And spoke on the phone every now and then. In some ways it was as if nothing had changed, but in other ways, everything had.

He could see her now. Almost whenever he wanted. And that was a miracle. Her knife wounds had healed up enough that he was able to take out the stitches. He wanted to take her back to the hospital to have it done, but Blythe had argued so vehemently, in the end he didn't make her.

And she was right. He was a paramedic and could remove them just as easily as a nurse or doctor at the hospital, and he wouldn't charge her an arm and a leg for the privilege. The slice on her hand was still healing, though, and would require more time to completely clear up.

Now he was at her house to pick her up for an official date. He shifted nervously on the front porch, waiting for Blythe to open the door.

When she did, Squirrel could only gape at her.

"Do I look okay?" she asked after several moments.

As if on autopilot, Squirrel took a step forward, put one hand on her hip and the other grasped her chin. He tilted her face up and leaned close. He brushed his lips across hers once, then twice. He hesitated, not wanting to pull back but knowing he should.

But Blythe moved first. She pressed her body into his and tilted her head, giving them both a better angle. Then her tongue brushed against his bottom lip.

That was all it took.

Squirrel didn't know who moaned, maybe they both did. But the next thing he knew, they were kissing as if this were the last kiss either of them would ever have before the world ended. Their tongues dueled and he felt her hands reach up behind his neck. She held him to her as they made out on the front porch.

One of Squirrel's hands was on her ass, holding her as close to his body as possible, and the other was tangled in her short dark hair, when the sound that had been niggling at his brain since they'd started kissing finally registered.

Reluctantly, he pulled back and grinned down at Blythe.

Her lips were swollen from his kisses, and she had a beautiful, deep flush on her face and upper neck. Her eyelids were at half-mast and she looked almost drugged.

Not able to help himself, Squirrel kissed her once more. A quick kiss with a swift brush of his tongue over her bottom lip. "Sounds like our friends approve," he said dryly when he pulled back.

Blythe blinked then turned her head toward the house next door.

He followed suit—and saw both Sophie and Chief standing by their front door, clapping.

He was worried Blythe would be mortified, but he sagged in relief when she held up her middle finger at the couple. They laughed.

"Have fun tonight, kids," Sophie called out.

"Don't do anything I wouldn't do," Chief added.

Blythe looked up at Squirrel after waving at their friends. "Hi."

"Hi," Squirrel echoed. "And in case my reaction didn't answer your question, you look amazing."

"Thanks."

Squirrel put his hands on her shoulders and held her away from him for a moment as he took her in. She was wearing a skirt that landed above her knees. It was a deep purple and was made of some sort of wispy fabric. It looked light and airy, and it easily swished around her legs as she moved. She'd topped it with a white V-neck blouse, which dipped low enough that he could easily see her cleavage. The shoulders were bare—it looked like they'd been cut out of the material—and the arms ended in three-quarter-length sleeves.

She'd obviously spent some time on her hair. It looked different than he'd ever seen it before. It was spiked up a little in the front and looked like it had been trimmed in the back. It had been uneven and a bit ragged before, but now it looked sleek and styled.

She had a bit of makeup on, her eyes looking bigger than ever. The hazel color of her irises popped with the eyeshadow and mascara she'd used. Her lips were a blush-rose color, and he wondered if he had lipstick all over his own lips. Not caring, he brought a hand up to her face and ran his thumb over the apple of her cheek. "You look good, baby. Really good."

"Sophie and Adeline came over earlier and helped me get ready."

"You should know, I've always been proud to have you by my side. You didn't have to get all dolled up for me."

"I did it for me," Blythe blurted, then looked away from him, as if embarrassed by what she'd admitted.

"Look at me," Squirrel said before he'd thought

about it. He was about to apologize for being so bossy, but she did as he asked and brought her eyes back to his. "Good for you," he said with a smile. "And that was mighty presumptuous of me to assume you put on makeup for *me*, huh?"

"It's just that...it's been so long since I've made any kind of effort with my appearance. There's just no time for that when you're hungry or trying to find a safe place to sleep."

"I understand. You don't have to justify to me or anyone else why you are or aren't wearing makeup. But anytime you want to make the effort, Blythe, I'm more than willing to take you out and show you off if that's what you want."

"That's not why—"

"I know it's not," Squirrel interrupted. "But I'm proud as fuck to have you by my side. I haven't ever dated anyone as beautiful as you. I've never been the guy others are jealous of. For the first time, I know I'm going to be envied. But I should warn you...since I've never been in this situation before, I can't guarantee how I'll react to other men staring at you. I've never been the jealous type before, but I have a feeling that'll change once I bring you out in public, looking like you do right now."

"Sawyer," Blythe complained, her cheeks pinkening again.

"It's true."

Her eyes met his. "I don't understand how you haven't already been snatched up by someone before now."

"Look at me," he said, dropping his hands from her and holding his arms out to his sides. "I'm not exactly centerfold material."

Squirrel forced himself to remain still as she did as he asked. He could feel her eyes studying him. Everywhere they touched, he swore he could feel her gaze as a physical caress. He knew what she'd see. He saw himself every day in the mirror. Short brown hair, glasses, a nose that was a bit too long, ears that stuck out a bit too much. Broad shoulders, but not broad enough to be especially noticed. Slender build.

Yup, time and time again, he'd been overlooked by women for sexier, taller, and more outwardly masculine men. He hadn't particularly cared in the past, but if Blythe rejected him, he would care. A lot.

He tensed when her unbandaged hand landed in the middle of this chest. She looked up at him and said quietly, "Do you want to know what I see when I look at you?"

Squirrel wanted to say no, he really was a chicken where she was concerned, but forced himself to nod. "Sure."

"I see a man who let a homeless woman keep his

cell phone because he wanted her to be safe." Her hand wandered up to his shoulder. "I see a man who I knew wanted me to accept his help, but didn't push the issue when I told him to drop it. I see a man who loves his family and would do anything to protect them. A man who values his friendships with the people he works with and works hard to cultivate those friendships. I see a selfless, proud, generous man."

Her words made him feel good, but at the same time, disappointed him somewhat. Squirrel wanted her to be attracted to his looks almost as much as he wanted her to like him for who he was.

He opened his mouth to thank her, but one of her fingers pressed against his lips, shushing him. Her voice dropped, became more seductive. "I see those traits in your friends too...but I'm not physically attracted to them, Sawyer. Not like I am to you. I wouldn't feel comfortable being with men like Cade and Chief because of their size. That's just never been my thing. But you turn me on so much, it's all I can do not to fall to my knees and undo your pants. I don't know what women you've been hanging around with, but you are one hell of a sexy man. When I was in high school, I dated the president of the chess club, did I tell you that already?"

Squirrel shook his head, fascinated by the woman standing in front of him.

"I did. I wasn't the most popular girl in school, not by a long shot, but I also wasn't exactly unpopular. I was on the soccer team and sometimes hung out with a couple of the cheerleaders. One of the football players asked me to prom one year, but I turned him down in favor of that chess club president. Ronald." She chuckled. "We went to prom but left half an hour later. We checked into a fancy hotel and spent the rest of the night in each other's arms. Want to know what I learned?"

Squirrel swallowed hard. On the one hand, he was kinda pissed she was talking about fucking another guy when she was practically in *his* arms, but on the other hand, the events she was describing took place over ten years ago. He wasn't exactly a virgin, he had no right to get upset with her... besides, she obviously had a point to make. So he nodded, not able to speak if his life depended on it.

"I learned that I'd much rather have a chess club president in my bed than a football player. My friends bragged about how big their jock boyfriends' dicks were. But when others weren't around, they admitted that they were never satisfied in bed. That the boys they slept with didn't even know what the word foreplay meant and they hardly ever got off when they were fucked."

Blythe plastered herself to Squirrel then and he grabbed her hips, holding her in place against him. He knew she could feel his rock-hard dick against her stomach, but he didn't care.

She reached up and put her arms around his shoulders. He felt her fingertips against his nape as she caressed him. "I couldn't relate to those girls at all. Because on prom night, that chess club president made me come four times. He knew exactly what to do with his tongue and fingers. He may not have had the biggest dick, but by the time he finally fucked me, I was so primed, I didn't give a shit."

Squirrel got what she was trying to say. Her words were a bit awkward—he didn't think she was trying to insinuate anything about the size of *his* dick—but all her talk about sex and foreplay had him more than ready to show her how much he appreciated her attempt at a pep talk.

He palmed her head and, fisting her short hair, tipped her head back and kissed her. Hard. Without worrying if he was pleasuring her. He took what he wanted.

But she was obviously pleased. He felt one of her legs hike up around his hip. He reached down with his free hand and held her leg up, keeping her open to him. He bent his knees a fraction until his cock was nestled between her legs. He pulled back from the kiss but didn't drop her leg. They stood there for thirty seconds, breathing hard and staring at each other.

Squirrel was a heartbeat away from shoving up her flimsy skirt and fucking her right there on her porch. Her fresh, flowery scent was heavy in his nostrils and he knew he'd never forget it. He'd buy whatever shower gel she used in bulk so she'd always smell that way and he could always remember this moment.

Taking a deep breath, Squirrel forced himself to let go of her leg, managing not to groan as it brushed against his thigh when she slowly brought it back to the ground.

"I haven't had any sexual thoughts for so long, I thought I was frigid," Blythe told him. "But you give me hope."

"I'm going to give you more than that," Squirrel told her with a growl. "And you're not frigid. Not even close."

She giggled. Squirrel wanted to roll his eyes at how adorable she was, but he didn't want to look away from her for one second. "You have a choice," he said.

"Yeah?"

"Yeah. You can turn around and invite me inside and I can show you exactly what *I* can do with my tongue. I guarantee you'll forget about that damn chess club guy in two seconds flat."

"Or?" she asked when he didn't say anything else.

"Or, you can turn around, lock your door, and let me take you out on a date like we planned."

"Can't we do both?" she asked, blinking innocently.

"Fuck," Squirrel said, tightening his grip on her body. Then he forced himself to relax and said seriously, "You got all dressed up. You look amazing. As much as I can't believe I'm saying this, I want to take you out. Besides, I have a surprise for you."

At his words, the sexual heat in her eyes dimmed and she looked excited. "A surprise? I love surprises, and I never get them. Well…good ones, that is."

"This is a good one," he reassured her. "At least, I hope you'll think so. I want you. I don't think *that's* any surprise."

She shook her head.

"But I want to continue to get to know you too. We've talked a lot on the phone. We know a lot about each other. But I want you to trust me. To know down to the marrow of your bones that I've got your back."

Blythe bit her lip. "I don't like to talk about how I

142

ended up on the streets. I'm embarrassed about it all."

He knew she'd understand what he was getting at. "I know, baby. But I need to know, so I can make sure it doesn't happen again."

"You can't guarantee that," she said sadly. "Sometimes things just happen."

"I can make sure of it," he countered. "*If* I know what happened."

Blythe sighed. "I made bad choices."

It was his turn to put his finger over her lips. "Let me take you out. Show you off. Make all the other men we run into jealous as fuck that you're with me. Let them wonder why a beautiful woman like you would be with a nerd like me. We'll talk. I'll reassure you. Then I'll give you your surprise. *Then*, if you still want, I'll come back here with you."

She licked her lips and the second her tongue touched his finger, his cock jerked with renewed lust.

"You have no idea how hard it was for me not to come into your room when I was staying over here with you. I wanted to gather you in my arms and tell you that everything would be all right."

"Is that all you wanted to do?" Blythe asked coyly.

"Fuck no. I wanted to kiss every inch of your body, if only to erase every mark those assholes put on you." He pulled her into his arms in a full-body hug. They were touching from thighs to chest. "There's no rush, baby. I would wait my entire life for a chance to be with you."

Without a word, Blythe pulled out of his arms and turned to the door. For a second, Squirrel's stomach clenched in disappointment that she'd turned away from him, but when she simply locked the door then came right back into his arms, he smiled. She'd made her decision, and he'd made his.

He'd make sure she knew she wasn't frigid if it was the last thing he did. And he'd start by helping her forget about Ronald what's-his-name by making her come at least *five* times when they did get together. No way some pansy-ass chess club president was making his girl come more times than he could.

CHAPTER NINE

*B*lythe stared across the table at Sawyer. She'd shocked herself tonight. She hadn't meant to tell him everything she had on the porch, but when he'd looked a bit unsure about himself, she couldn't stand for him to think for even a second she wasn't attracted to him.

Sure, he wasn't as "in your face" alpha as the others were, but from talking to him for months and getting to know him in person over the last few weeks, it was more than obvious to her that he was as masculine as his fellow firefighters.

He wouldn't take no for an answer when it had to do with her wellbeing. There was the time her groceries had gotten low, but she kept telling him she was fine and didn't need anything. He took it upon himself to shop for her and had brought over literally twenty bags filled with food.

Then there was the time the detective had wanted to meet with her, and she'd asked Sophie if she could drive her to the police station. Apparently, she'd told Chief, who in turn had told Squirrel about the meeting. He'd shown up at the house to take her to the appointment and refused to sit in the waiting room while she spoke with Detective Nelson about the investigation. He'd been by her side when the detective had admitted they'd had no luck so far, tracking down Dog or Tweek.

She remembered the evening she and Sawyer were texting and she'd admitted that she wasn't having a good night. She'd been thinking too much about what had happened, about her nights on the street, and about her mom, and knew she wouldn't be able to sleep. He'd called her and refused to hang up. They'd talked for four hours, until she'd practically fallen asleep with the phone in her hand. The last thing she remembered was his husky voice telling her to sleep well.

Yeah, he might look like a chess club president, but his outer body didn't match his pit bull, alpha interior. But she liked the way he looked. Blythe could admit that she'd be intimidated to date someone like his friends. She liked all of them, but she'd constantly be comparing her own average looks to his if he was the stereotypical "tall, dark, and handsome."

Their kisses had been intense on her porch, but their discussion was even more so. She hadn't exaggerated; she hadn't thought about sex for many years. But recently she couldn't think of anything else. At least when she was around Sawyer.

"How's your lasagna?" Sawyer asked her, bringing her out of her head.

"Excellent. How's yours?"

"The chicken is amazing. Want a bite?" he asked.

Blythe nodded, and he speared a piece of chicken and held it out for her. Leaning forward, she didn't take her eyes from Sawyer's. It seemed intimate, him feeding her, but she liked the feeling. A lot.

Apparently, he did too, as she saw his pupils dilate as he watched her chew.

"Good?" he asked in a low, husky voice.

Blythe swallowed. She'd hardly tasted it. How could she with the way he was looking at her? "Yeah."

Somehow, she made it through the rest of the dinner. They'd shared a piece of cheesecake for dessert and had been making small talk when Blythe blurted, "My mom died."

The smile that had been on Sawyer's face disappeared and he got up from the other side of the intimate booth and came around to hers. She automatically scooted over, giving him room, and he sat next to her. One of his arms rested on the seatback behind her, and he placed his other hand on her thigh. "I'm so sorry, Blythe."

"She'd been sick for a while. Cancer. At first, it looked like she was going to beat it. She went through chemo and was doing better. But then it came back. I worked at Caterpillar on one of the assembly lines, but the factory was on the other side of the city from where I lived with Mom. I had arranged to work a lot of half days, but by the time I got Mom back home from her treatments, it was too late to manage even that. I ultimately missed work too many times and was fired. Then I sold my car to try to pay for the drugs Mom needed. Eventually, we simply ran out of money. By then, my mom was dying. I spent her last days telling her how much I loved her and not to worry about me. She knew I was broke, and she worried so much."

Blythe took a deep breath. This next part was harder. "She died on a Tuesday, and my landlord told me if I didn't have the three months' rent I owed him by Friday afternoon, he was kicking me out."

"Jesus," Sawyer breathed. "What a dick."

"I can't totally blame him," Blythe countered. "I'd

been trying to pay him the back-rent in installments, but it wasn't enough. I could tell he was getting more and more irritated with the money situation. I mean, he had to make a living too; letting me stay rent-free just because my mom was sick wasn't exactly a good business decision. He did let me stay until Mom…" Her voice trailed off and she struggled to get herself under control. "Anyway, I sold as much as I could around the apartment to pay for Mom to be cremated. I came home on Friday after getting her ashes and my key didn't work in the lock."

She felt Sawyer's feather-light touch on her thigh. His thumb moved back and forth, telling her without words that he was there. It helped. A lot.

Blythe finished her sob story. "I had about forty bucks in my purse. No car. No clothes other than what I was wearing. My landlord put all my stuff on the curb and it had already been picked through by the neighbors. I couldn't afford to put what was left in storage, so I had to leave it all there. I knew I'd have better luck downtown than out in the suburbs. I mean, it's not like there were shelters on every street corner where I lived. I took a cab downtown and was lucky in that the first homeless shelter I went to, I got in. I wasn't always that lucky though. If you don't get there right when they open in the afternoon, it's likely the beds will be gone. I was given some clothes and my backpack from one of the ladies at that first shelter, and that was that. I was officially homeless."

"How long?" Sawyer asked quietly.

"About a year," Blythe told him, not wanting to think about how long she'd been on the streets. "At first I tried hard to get help. But between bad luck and having to cancel the few interviews I'd managed to set up, I was demoralized. I got depressed about everything and stopped trying... and that's on me. But the thing is, even if I hadn't lost my job and car in the first place, I wouldn't have been able to pay the medical bills. Mom literally owed over a hundred thousand dollars. I still can't pay that, obviously." She looked up at him. "Even if I get a job now, I'll still have to pay it, won't I?"

"I don't know," Sawyer told her immediately. "I'm sorry. But I bet we could talk to Beth and she could research it for us."

Blythe smiled. *Us.* She liked that. "I'll talk to her," she told him.

"What'd you do with your mom's ashes?" Sawyer asked.

She liked that he remembered that part of the story. "There's a green space on the west side of downtown called Milam Park. Do you know it?"

"Yeah, baby, I know it. That's near the abandoned building you lived in for a while, right?"

"Yes. I know it's probably illegal, but I took her there. Over several weeks, I spread her ashes in the park. I think she would've loved it."

"I know she would've."

"And…this may sound stupid, but I figured if I spread her ashes there, I could visit her from time to time. It's not the same as having a headstone in a cemetery, but it was the best I could do."

Sawyer leaned forward and brushed his lips against her temple before saying, "You did good, Blythe. What else?"

She looked up at him in confusion. "What else, what?"

Now *he* looked confused. "You said you were embarrassed about what happened that led you to being homeless. I'm wondering what else happened to get you there."

She shrugged. "I guess that's it."

Now Sawyer looked angry. "Blythe, you have absolutely nothing to be embarrassed about."

"Sawyer, I lost my job. My car. My landlord locked me out of my apartment because I hadn't paid rent in months. He promised that he'd work with me after I told him about my mom, but the measly payments I'd managed to throw his way didn't cut it.

I guess I should be happy he waited until after Mom died before evicting me. I wandered around on the streets for months. I still have no money, nothing I own is something I've bought for myself. Even what I'm wearing right now, someone else had to purchase for me. I'm just as pathetic now as I was then, except now I'm not sleeping under trash bins or in shelters."

Now he *really* looked pissed. "Stop it," he ordered. "You aren't pathetic, not even close. You did everything you could for your mom. You ensured she died in a familiar place, with you by her side. You're selfless and loving, and I know she was so thankful that you were there for her. You lost everything not because you were selfish or a bitch. You lost it all because you were exactly the opposite."

Blythe swallowed hard but didn't look away from him as he continued.

"What if Sophie was in your same situation? Or Adeline? Or Beth? Would you think they were pathetic? Would you offer them food, clothes, a place to stay?" He paused as if waiting for her response.

"You know I would," Blythe said softly.

"And would you think they were pathetic if they'd ended up homeless through no fault of their own?"

She shook her head this time.

"Right. So why in the world would you think that of yourself? Blythe, you're amazing. Your time on the streets could've hardened you. You could've turned to drugs, robbery, or prostitution to get the things you needed to survive. But you didn't. You simply suffered without. That night you were attacked, you could've ignored what was happening. Tweek and Dog didn't even know you were there. But you didn't. You put yourself in the middle of the situation to protect and save others."

"Remember when I called you…and told you about Milena and her friend being kidnapped from that nightclub?"

"Of course."

"That was *my* fault, Sawyer. I told that guy where she would be. I handed them over to him on a silver platter."

Sawyer cocked his head. "Why?"

"Why what?"

"Why did you do it?"

"Tell him where to find them?"

"Yeah."

"Because he'd kidnapped Billy. He's only seven. I'd met him and his mom at one of the shelters. She was trying so hard to get back on her feet. The guy said he'd tell me where he'd stashed him if I told him where Milena would be. The cops didn't believe me, and I couldn't get him on tape admitting he'd kidnapped Billy. I tried to get back to the club to tell Milena to be careful, but it was too late."

"Right. So you told that asshole where Milena was, you rescued a little boy, you went back to the club to try to warn Milena, and then you called *me* to give me a head's up that she and her friend had been taken…and you think you're a bad person?"

When he put it that way, Blythe wasn't sure what to say. "I can't find her," she blurted.

"Find who?"

"Hope. And her son. I've looked everywhere. It's like they've disappeared into thin air. I'm so worried about them, and somehow I feel as if it's my fault they're missing."

"Listen to me," Sawyer said. He turned her so one of her knees was hiked up on the bench seat as she faced him. His hands were on her shoulders and he looked at her intently. "It's not your fault; they have to be *somewhere*. And shit happened to you. It sucks. Still sucks. I'm sorry about your mom. But I know without a doubt she'd be super proud of you. You're going to get back on your feet. It might take a while, and there will be highs and lows as you do it, but you *will* make it."

"How can you be so sure?"

"Because I know you, Blythe. You have a core of

strength inside you that I haven't seen in many people in my lifetime. And besides that, you have me. And Beth. And Sophie and Adeline. Not to mention all the firefighters."

"But I don't know them and they don't know me."

Sawyer laughed then. Threw his head back and guffawed as if she'd said the funniest thing he'd ever heard. When he'd gotten himself under control, he said, "Baby, they know you."

"How? I don't even think I've met them all yet."

"Because I talk about you all the time. They're actually sick of me talking about you. I've been doing it for months. They know you, Blythe. Not only that, but they like you."

She gaped at him with wide eyes.

"Fuck, you're adorable," Sawyer said, then leaned forward slowly, giving her time to understand what he was about to do, and reject him if she needed to.

But Blythe didn't want to reject him. One of the only places she felt safe was when she was with him. Specifically, when she was in his arms.

She lifted her chin, meeting him halfway. The moment their lips touched, Blythe felt her worries fade. She still didn't have any money. All her clothes were given to her by others. The food she ate was charity. Even the roof over her head wasn't hers. But none of that mattered right at this moment.

Sawyer's belief in her meant the world to Blythe. There were many times over the last few months when she felt as if she were nobody. As if she'd never feel normal again. But Sawyer's words, and his lips on her own, made her believe, if only for the moment, that she was the old Blythe again.

Tilting her head to get more of him, Blythe brought her hand up to his face. She rested it on his cheek and took what he gave her. He pulled back a fraction but didn't take his hands from the sides of her neck where they'd moved when he'd kissed her.

"You okay?"

Licking her lips and tasting the chocolate sauce from the cheesecake they'd eaten, Blythe nodded.

"You up for more or do you want to go home?"

Home. What a wonderful word. Even if Sophie's house wasn't exactly home, it was more of a home than she'd had for the last year or so. "I thought you had a surprise for me," she said.

"I do. But it can wait if you've had enough. I'm more than happy to sit on the couch and watch TV with you if you'd prefer."

Blythe thought about it for a nanosecond. "I want my surprise."

He smiled at her. "Then that's what you'll get. And I have to say...I like seeing you like this."

"Like what?"

"Excited. Happy."

"I like feeling like this."

Sawyer kissed her again, a quick peck that made Blythe long for more. Then he scooted out of the booth and held out his hand for her.

Placing her uninjured hand in his, she let him pull her up and out of the booth. He held her hand as he paid for their meal, and as he pushed the door open for her.

Blythe knew the smile on her face was probably dorky, but she didn't care. She couldn't remember the last time she'd been happy. Truly happy.

CHAPTER TEN

"*S*awyer, no."

Squirrel shut off the engine and turned to face Blythe. He knew this was going to be hard for her, but his sisters had been bugging him constantly for the last couple weeks. They wanted to meet her and wouldn't take no for an answer. He'd been putting them off, wanting Blythe to settle in a bit more, but they were done waiting and told him in no uncertain terms to bring her by the house, or they'd figure out how to meet her on their own.

"They want to meet you, baby," he said gently.

Blythe shook her head, her eyes wide with panic.

He reached over and put a hand on either side of her head. "What are you afraid of?"

Her mouth opened, then closed, then opened again.

"Let me guess. You're afraid they'll judge you for being homeless. You're afraid they aren't going to like you in person. You're afraid they'll disapprove of you dating me. Right?"

She nodded.

He smiled at her. "Blythe, they don't give a shit that you were homeless. To them, it doesn't mean a whole lot. They're going to love you—hell, they *already* love you. Natalie texts you more than she does me. When she was arguing with Mom about something recently, I told her to ask you what *you* thought. When you told her the same thing Mom did, she accepted it without question. Emma admires you so much, you have no idea. She told me the other day that she's considering double majoring in pre-med and sociology in college. She wants to be a doctor, but she also wants to make sure she can help when someone's in a situation like you were."

Blythe gaped up at him, obviously shocked.

"They know all about your situation, baby. I don't keep things from my family. I was worried about you and told them you had my phone and that I was concerned about you living on the streets. They encouraged me to find you and take you home, as if you were a stray dog or something." He chuckled. "They were as happy as I was when you moved into Sophie's house. Trust them. Trust *me*," he said. "This is supposed to be a happy surprise. I thought you'd like to meet them."

"I do...I would...I just... I'm nervous."

"I get that. But you have absolutely no reason to be. How about this? If things become too much, just let me know. I'll get you out of there and I'll take you home immediately. Okay?"

She took a deep breath. "Okay. I trust you."

Her words made a warm feeling flow out from his heart to the rest of his body. Her trust meant the world. He leaned over and kissed her forehead tenderly before climbing out of the vehicle and meeting her at the front. They walked hand in hand up to the door.

Before they arrived, it swung open and his youngest sister was running toward them. Natalie threw herself into his arms, forcing him to let go of Blythe. He twirled her around in a circle and smiled as she laughed. The second he put her back on her feet, she turned to Blythe. Throwing her arms around her as well, Natalie started babbling.

"It's so good to meet you! I've been wanting to meet you for soooo long! Your advice about that boy was spot on. I think he was just talking to me to try to make this other girl jealous, which wasn't cool." She pulled back but didn't stop talking. "How are you? You look good. Sawyer told me what happened.

Well, some of it. He said you were hurt. That sucks. Does your hand hurt? Can I see it? I heard you walloped the other guy big time. That's awesome!"

"Take a breath, Nat," Squirrel admonished. "And give her some breathing room."

"Whatever," the teenager said, rolling her eyes at her brother. Then she grabbed Blythe's unbandaged hand and dragged her toward the door. "Come on. Em and Charlotte are inside and they can't wait to meet you too. Did you eat? Mom made a buttload of food even though Sawyer told her you guys were going out before you came over here. Don't feel bad if you can't eat it, although my mom's chocolate chip peanut butter Butterfinger cookies are awesome."

Squirrel trailed along behind his sister and Blythe with a huge smile on his face. Leave it to his youngest sister to steamroll over everything and take charge. He loved that about her.

When he caught up to them, he put his hand on the small of Blythe's back. She looked over her shoulder and gave him a wobbly smile. He wasn't sure what she was thinking, but he hoped she was merely overwhelmed with Natalie's welcome and not having second thoughts.

Leaning forward, he whispered in her ear, "You okay?"

Blythe nodded, but didn't have a chance to say anything as Natalie was dragging her inside.

Squirrel stood back and watched his family work their magic on Blythe. Emma and Charlotte greeted her as if she were their long-lost sister. Everyone was talking a mile a minute, going out of their way to make her feel welcome. His dad was next. He shook Blythe's hand warmly, giving her his trademark huge smile. He even went so far as to tell her that she was welcome at their house anytime.

Then it was his mom's turn. She didn't even hesitate to engulf Blythe in one of her mom hugs. He saw her whisper something in Blythe's ear, and Squirrel was going to intervene when he saw tears spring to Blythe's eyes, but he relaxed when she pulled back and smiled at his mom. Whatever his mother said had made Blythe emotional, but she wasn't immediately asking to leave, so he'd take that as a win.

Like Natalie promised, his mom had made a ton of food...even though she knew he was taking Blythe out to eat before they came over to the house. His sisters filled their plates with food though, and everyone went into the large living room to settle in and eat. Squirrel claimed Blythe before anyone else could and seated her on one end of their huge couch. He sat next to her and Charlotte grabbed the seat next to him. His dad took his customary spot in the recliner and the others settled in the other available seats.

As they ate, Blythe gamely answered his sisters' questions as best she could. But she also questioned them right back. Asked Emma about her college plans. Talked to Charlotte about the dance she'd been to. Encouraged Natalie when she went on and on about the boys she liked and which she thought liked her back.

She was also awesome with his parents. When his dad started talking about his marketing job, she didn't hesitate to jump in with questions and let him know how impressed she was with the few advertisements she'd seen from the campaigns he'd worked on. His mom had been somewhat quiet, but Blythe drew her out too, getting her to talk about her job as an executive with USAA, the insurance and financial services institution.

After dinner, Natalie and Charlotte took everyone's plates back to the kitchen and returned with a huge platter of the cookies his mom had made. Everyone was relaxed and mellow and Squirrel was feeling good about how the night was going.

Then Natalie had to bring up the one topic he'd warned her, repeatedly, not to bring up.

"I didn't know you were homeless when we first started texting."

"Nat," Squirrel warned.

But Blythe put her hand on his arm and said, "It's okay. It's not like you *would* know unless I had said something, Natalie."

"You're the first homeless person I've ever met."

Squirrel watched as Blythe took a deep breath before she answered. "I doubt that."

Natalie's brows came down in confusion. "What do you mean?"

"It's not like people wear signs that say 'I sleep in my car' or 'I don't have any food at home.' I bet there are some kids at your school whose parents have had money issues and either don't have a stable place to live, or are struggling with affording the things they need for their everyday life."

Natalie was his easy-going sister. The one who never really got sad. She could talk a mile a minute and always saw things with a positive eye. For the first time in a long time, Squirrel could see her really thinking about what someone had said.

"Really?"

"Really," Blythe affirmed. "Think about it. I'm sure you've seen kids turn down lunch, saying they're not hungry. Maybe they really aren't hungry…but maybe they simply can't afford to buy the food at the school or to bring their own. What about the kids who are made fun of because their clothes are dirty or smelly? Do you think they really want to come to school that way? Do you think they *like* being made fun of? It costs money to wash clothes."

"There's a girl in my English class. Everyone thinks she's weird. She sits in the back of the class by herself and doesn't talk much. It's like you said, she wears the same clothes all the time and they usually look dirty. Her hair is always up in a baseball cap, and when the teacher makes her take it off, her hair is really greasy looking."

"Have you talked to her? Asked her how she's doing?"

Natalie looked aghast. "No way!"

"Why?" Blythe wasn't letting his sister out of the conversation. Everyone else was silent, listening.

"Well…because she's weird."

"Is she? How do you know if you haven't talked to her?"

Natalie looked down at her lap and picked at a string hanging off her shirt. "I don't want my friends to make fun of me like they do her."

Blythe nodded, then said, "Most of the time when

I was homeless, people would look right through me. They'd pretend they didn't see me. I smelled, my clothes were dirty, but that never made me less of a person, Nat. I still felt sad, happy, frustrated, or embarrassed. Then one day, a woman looked right at me and smiled. She said good morning. She told me I had beautiful eyes. Then she handed me a bag that had a blueberry muffin in it. I didn't say much back to her because I was trying to process the fact that this pretty woman, who I had never met, was being nice to me.

"To this day, I'll never forget how good that first muffin tasted. If I had the same thing today, I'd probably find it wasn't nearly as good as the cookies your mom made tonight, but at that point in time, when I was hungry, depressed, and trying really hard to remember that I was a good person, it was the best thing I'd ever eaten."

Squirrel hated this. *Hated* it. For the millionth time, he mentally beat himself up for not forcing Blythe to accept his help before she'd been hurt.

She obviously felt him tense next to her because she rested her hand on his leg, her fingers on the inside of his thigh, her thumb gently caressing. If he'd been anywhere else, if they were talking about anything else, Squirrel might've thought she was coming on to him. But he knew she was simply trying to comfort him. Even as she talked about the most difficult time in her life, *she* was comforting *him*.

"I was at rock bottom that day. I felt as if I was an awful human being. I was depressed and at the end of my rope. But all it took was one person looking *at* me, and not *through* me, to get me through that day."

"Did you ever see her again?" Natalie asked.

"Yup. All the time. But I never really talked to her. I didn't feel like I was *good* enough to talk to her. So, I hid whenever she came around. But I watched her. She treated my friends Tadd and Louise as if they were her good friends. She took care of them, but never forgot about me. She always brought me a muffin, even though I wouldn't talk to her and hid in the abandoned building I was living in whenever she came around."

"Wow."

"Yeah. And you know what else?"

"What?"

"I now live in her old place. She lives next door with her man-friend, and she also let Tadd and Louise live in her house before me. My point is…if Sophie hadn't reached out to me, to let me know that she saw *me*—not a dirty, worthless homeless person—I might not be here today."

"Man-friend?" Emma asked.

Blythe chuckled, and while Squirrel wasn't quite ready to laugh, not when he'd just learned how close the woman he wanted for his own had been to giving up, his lips did twitch at his sister's question.

"If you ever met Chief, you'd never think of him as a boy. There's no way I could ever call him a *boy*friend," Blythe told his sister.

Everyone laughed, except for Natalie.

"Her name is Kodie," Natalie said quietly.

"Who?" Blythe asked.

"The girl in my class. The one who sits in the back." Natalie was sitting on the floor at Blythe's feet, her legs crossed. His sister tilted her head back and looked straight into Blythe's eyes and said, "I'm going to talk to her tomorrow. It's not her fault she smells and seems weird. Maybe she's like you and just needs a friend."

"And what if your friends don't like you talking to her? What if they laugh at *you*? Don't get her hopes up, Natalie. If you're nice to her, then back off because you don't want to make your friends mad, then she's better off if you leave her alone. You don't want her to think she's the butt of your jokes or something. There's nothing worse than getting someone's hopes up then cruelly dashing them."

Natalie nodded seriously. "I'll explain to my

friends. We'll all talk to Kodie. The only one who might not like it is Aimee, but she's mean to everyone, so it won't matter if she doesn't want to do it. We don't need her anyway."

Blythe leaned forward and rested her elbows on her knees as she stared at Natalie. Squirrel couldn't stop his hand from moving to the small of her back as if his life depended on it. Her shirt rode up and his fingers landed on her warm skin. He wanted to caress her there, move his hand up under her shirt and trace her backbone. Wanted to dip his fingers down inside the waistband of her skirt, but he refrained. Barely.

"You're a good person, Natalie. Kodie is one lucky girl. I hope it works out. Don't be surprised if she rebuffs you at first. She probably won't trust that you have good intentions. Keep at her. She probably needs a friend more than you know."

"I'll be her friend," Natalie vowed.

Blythe sat back, and Squirrel shifted his hand to her thigh. He loved when she covered his hand with her own.

"How'd you end up on the streets?" his dad asked softly.

Squirrel stiffened yet again. Blythe had just told *him* the circumstances that had led to her being homeless; it was way too soon for his family to be asking.

He opened his mouth to tell his dad to back off, but as usual, Blythe got there before he could say anything.

"My mom got sick. Cancer. I took care of her, and eventually lost my job because there were a few too many days she felt so bad, I couldn't leave her. I sold everything I had of value to pay for her meds." She shrugged. "After she died, I got kicked out of my apartment because I was so far behind in the rent."

"Common decency is all but gone these days," his dad muttered.

"Was it hard?" Charlotte blurted.

"Was what hard?" Blythe asked.

"Living on the streets. I mean, you slept at the shelters most nights, right? And they had food?"

"Let me tell you about the shelters," Blythe said quietly. "If you're not there right when they open, you won't get a bed. You have no idea who slept on the cot you're lying on. Yes, the sheets are washed every day, but the mattresses themselves are old and dirty. You sleep in a room with at least ten other people. They do separate the women from the men, which is good, but that doesn't mean that desperate women won't steal from you. They do. Before I learned to use my backpack as a pillow, I had my stuff rifled through, and clothes and socks stolen from me as I slept.

"You never sleep real deeply, either, because you're always on alert. It's often unbearably hot in the shelters. Air conditioning costs money—money the shelters almost never have. And the food...it's barely edible most days. Don't get me wrong, I was grateful for it because if I didn't eat there, most of the time I didn't eat at all, but the hot food is usually cold, and the cold food is usually hot. The volunteers aren't cooks, and they don't really know how to make such large quantities of food taste good.

"The shelters are depressing places, Charlotte. They do a lot of good, but there's not enough help, not enough people who really care about the homeless to operate them. Many people are there for their own agendas...for community service for some crime they did, or because they need volunteer hours for their job or school. Not to mention, a lot of homeless men and women are mentally unstable. They aren't taking the medicines they need in order to be functional or they're on hard drugs."

"Were you scared?" Emma asked.

"Every day," Blythe said softly. "Every damn day."

Squirrel wanted to end the conversation. Wanted to haul Blythe into his arms and tell her that he'd make sure she never had to go back there. But her words were having an impact on his family. He could tell they were extremely moved by her experiences and what she was sharing. His sisters were seeing a side of life they'd never really thought about before. It was good for them, even if it was painful to hear Blythe's story.

His mom got up from her spot on the couch and walked over to them. She looked down at Squirrel and motioned with her head for him to scoot over. Knowing better than to disobey his mom, Squirrel reluctantly moved over and gave his mom some room.

She sat right next to Blythe and put her hand on her knee. "You will never, ever be homeless again, honey. You need a place to go? You come here. If you're hungry? You call me and I'll make sure you have a nice big casserole. You might be Sawyer's friend, but I'm officially unofficially adopting you. You can have his old room. I think he might still have a poster of Marilyn Monroe under the bed up there."

"Mom," Squirrel complained, not really caring that she was airing his dirty laundry, not when her words made Blythe smile.

"I don't know what to say," Blythe told his mom.

"You don't have to say anything, honey," she replied. "All you need to do is promise that you'll come here if you ever find yourself in a situation like that again. I'm so sorry about you losing your mother, but the fact that you did everything in your power to make sure she was as comfortable as she could be, says everything that needs to be said about the kind of person you are."

"Thank you," Blythe choked out.

Squirrel watched as his mom reached out and hauled Blythe into her arms. They hugged for a long minute before his mom finally sat back. She stood and motioned to Squirrel to return to his previous position at Blythe's side.

Shaking his head at how ridiculously cute his mom could be, Squirrel did as ordered. This time his hand wrapped around Blythe's waist and he pulled her into his side.

"Okay, time to wrap this up," his mom declared. "I'm sure Blythe and Sawyer have better things to do than sit around here all night."

As his sisters protested their departure, Squirrel leaned into Blythe. "You okay?"

She nodded but didn't say anything.

Squirrel kept his eye on her as she stood and hugged each of his sisters and reassured them that she'd be back soon. Then they each said their good-byes to his parents and were back in his Jeep and headed to her house before too long.

Blythe was silent throughout the ride, and Squirrel didn't push her. He wanted to reassure himself that she really was all right, but he didn't want to be driving when he did it.

He pulled into her driveway and cut off the engine. "Can I come in?" he asked when Blythe still didn't say anything.

She turned to him then. He thought she looked a little pale, but otherwise didn't show any outward signs of being in distress. But she was. How he knew that, Squirrel wasn't sure.

"I'd like that," she said softly.

They both got out and made their way to the door. Blythe unlocked it and Squirrel followed her inside.

"I'm going to go change…if that's okay?"

"Of course it is, baby. You want something to drink?"

"Ice water, please."

Squirrel nodded and narrowed his eyes as she walked away from him toward the master bedroom. He got down a glass and filled it with ice and water then went into the small living room. He put the water on the coffee table and waited for Blythe to return.

She came back into the room minutes later wearing

a pair of black leggings and his Station 7 T-shirt. It fell to mid-thigh on her and was huge. Without a word, she came to the couch and sat. Then she surprised him by bringing her legs up and curling herself into his side.

Squirrel wrapped his arm around her, holding her close. He felt her sigh, her warm breath wafting over his chest. He could feel it through the material of his shirt.

"Talk to me," he ordered.

"About what?"

"About how you're doing. About what you're thinking and feeling. Are you completely freaked out by my family? My sisters are nosy but they mean well. And my parents didn't mean to overstep, they were just concerned about you."

Blythe looked up at him then. "I'm not upset about anything your family said tonight."

"Then what's wrong?"

Blythe put her head back on his shoulder and sighed again. "I'm envious. You are so lucky to have such wonderful people in your life. Your sisters are delightful and your parents are so accepting and nice. There were so many times when my mom was sick, I wished for a sibling who could help me. Or a close friend I could call and bitch to. But I didn't have either. You'll never be alone in your life. You'll always have someone you can call up and say, 'I've had enough. I need help.'"

Squirrel shifted, putting one hand behind her neck as the other palmed the side of her head. He looked her straight in the eyes, wanting her to hear the sincerity behind his words. "And you'll never be alone again. I think you know when it comes to us, I want more. But even if we don't work out. Even if you decide down the line that I'm too nerdy, or bossy, or whatever…you'll have my family. I didn't always appreciate how important family was. It was just me and mom until I was in middle school and she remarried. I didn't like sharing her with anyone else, but my stepfather won me over with his constant love and support. Then when Emma was born and I saw how happy my mom was, I realized that family wasn't about blood, it was about so much more.

"My mom wasn't feeding you a line tonight. She's pretty much adopted you. You'll always be welcome over there, regardless of where the two of us stand. You need anything, all you have to do is call her, and she'll drop everything and be there for you.

"Not only that, but you don't seem to understand what it means to be part of a firefighter family. Every one of the firefighters has your back. Their women have your back. Hell, even Tadd and Louise have your back. You. Are. Not. Alone. Not ever again. Even if I do something so stupid you never want to see me again, they will still be your friends."

"Why do you do that?"

Squirrel blinked. "Do what?"

"Belittle yourself? I'm just as likely to do something that will make you wonder why you spend so much time and energy trying to rescue me."

Squirrel laughed for the first time since the intense conversation at his parents' house. "Baby, I know a good thing when I have it. There's nothing you could do that would make me decide I don't want you in my arms and bed anymore."

She stared at him. "What if I cheated on you?"

"*Are* you going to cheat on me?"

"That's not what I asked," she said stubbornly.

Squirrel tried to understand what she wasn't saying. "I haven't looked twice at another woman since the day you came up to me at the fire and I gave you my sweatshirt. You think I give every random woman my clothes when I'm working? And don't answer that. I don't. A Playboy Bunny could march her happy ass in front of me right now and I wouldn't even care. I find black leggings that mold to every inch of my girl's legs, and her wearing my T-shirt, a hell of a lot sexier."

She looked skeptical.

"You don't believe me?"

She shook her head as much as she could in his hold.

Squirrel deliberately looked down at her chest, smiling when he saw her nipples poking through the thin material. "All I can imagine is what you look like under this. I don't know what it is about a woman wearing a man's clothes, but it's sexy as fuck. Maybe because I know your naked tits are touching the same material my chest has touched. I can see your nipples hard as rocks under it. I can't wait to know what you'll taste like."

"Sawyer," she complained, even as she squirmed in his grasp.

"To answer your question, if you cheat on me, yeah, that would end our relationship. Just as I'd assume would happen if I ever cheated on you. But, baby, it's my responsibility to make sure you don't *want* to cheat on me."

"How?"

"It's my job to make you feel beautiful every day. It's my job to tell you how much I appreciate you. It's my job to put you first whenever I can. Yes, there will be times I have to work and I can't give you the attention you might need or want, but when I'm off shift, I'll do everything in my power to make sure you know how much I enjoy being with you. It's my job to listen to you when you're upset and need to bitch about something. To be there for you when you need a good cry. I'll gladly watch chick-flicks, and come get you if you call because you have a flat tire. None of that is a hardship. *None* of it. But if I'm doing all of that, and you still go out and sleep with another man behind my back, then yeah, we'll be done."

Blythe simply stared at him.

"I might not be the best-looking man out there. I might not be the man women dream of when they're fantasizing about their dream man. But I'll make damn sure you'll always have enough to eat, you'll have a roof over your head, a soft bed, and a safe place to sleep every night where you don't have to worry about anyone stealing your belongings or assaulting you."

She moved then, surprising Squirrel when he was lying flat on his back on the couch before he knew what had happened. Blythe straddled his stomach, her hands resting on his shoulders as if she could hold him in place.

Worried about her palm, even though it was much better by now, Squirrel immediately eased her down so she was resting her forearms on his chest rather than her hands.

"I'm not going to cheat on you," she told him

fiercely. "Why in the world would I want to? There's nothing about you I don't like. Your friends, your passion about your job, your family, your integrity, your sense of humor...I could go on and on."

"And I'm not going to cheat on *you*, so why are we even having this insane conversation?" he asked, narrowing his eyes up at her.

"I have no idea," she admitted. "What were we even talking about?" She smiled down at him.

The smile did him in. He'd been on pins and needles tonight, wishing he'd waited longer to bring her to his parents' house. Wishing he'd made sure they were good with each other before she had to bring up the touchy subject of her homelessness.

Slowly, giving her time to pull back, Squirrel lifted his head. But instead of moving back, Blythe met him halfway, just as she'd done earlier.

Their kiss was passionate and tender at the same time. A promise.

Squirrel forced himself to pull away before he was ready. She sighed and gave him her weight, her head landing on his shoulder, her nose nuzzling the skin of his neck.

Wrapping an arm around her, Squirrel closed his eyes and enjoyed the moment. He hadn't lied to her earlier. The second she'd wandered into the room in her leggings and his shirt, he'd gotten hard. She was so damn sexy, he still couldn't believe he was there with her. She wasn't perfect—she was still too thin, had circles under her eyes, and still looked under-nourished—but to him, she was beautiful. What she'd been through made her that way. Her person-ality made her that way. Her loyalty, her tenacity, her ability to see the good in people. There was so much about her that he liked and admired, it made her the perfect woman...for *him*.

She had her faults. She was a bit too pessimistic about herself—not that he was one to talk—and didn't trust or ask for help easily. But she was getting better with those things day by day.

They stayed together on the couch for quite a while. Squirrel thought Blythe had fallen asleep on top of him. Her slow, even breaths against his neck were both comforting and arousing. He should've been embarrassed about the condition of his dick, she had to feel how hard he was, but he wasn't. It seemed natural. Besides, he was always hard around her. She might as well get used to it now.

"Stay?" she whispered.

"Anything you want," he whispered back.

"I want you," was her quiet reply.

Squirrel closed his eyes and sighed. When she didn't say anything else, he opened his eyes and peered at her. This time, she was asleep. He didn't know if she was actually fully awake when she'd said the words, but he'd never forget them.

She wanted him. *Him*. Squirrel. The nerd. The man everyone always overlooked.

He'd make sure she never regretted choosing him. Not for one second.

CHAPTER ELEVEN

*B*lythe walked out of the small public library and immediately pulled out her phone. It was instinctive. The first person she wanted to share her news with was Sawyer.

Blythe: *You around?*

　Squirrel: *I'm here, baby. How'd it go?*

　Blythe: *I got it! She offered me the job right on the spot after my interview!*

　Squirrel: *Fantastic! I told you! I knew you had it in the bag.*

　Blythe: *In the bag? Who says that?*

　Squirrel: *I do. Proud of you.*

· · ·

Blythe stared down at the phone. "Proud of you." She re-read the words over and over again. Sawyer was proud of her. Shit, she was proud of herself. The job wasn't exactly the end of all her worries. It paid minimum wage and wasn't even full-time, but it was something.

She was starting next week, restocking shelves in the library near Sophie's house. She could walk to work, so she didn't need a car yet. She'd work from eight in the morning until one, Monday through Thursday.

Apparently, she took too long to text Sawyer back, because her phone vibrated with another incoming text.

Squirrel: We'll celebrate tonight. I get off shift at five. I'll be home at 5:30. We're going out.

Blythe: It's not that big of a deal. It's only part-time. And minimum wage.

Squirrel: Bullshit. It's the start of your comeback. It's a huge deal. 5:30.

Home. He said he'd be *home* at five-thirty. Ever since the night she'd met his parents, he'd been staying at her house every night again. He'd given her some space after she'd first moved in, but she loved having him back.

It felt safer, more comfortable...*right* with him there. Blythe didn't like being dependent on anyone, but Sawyer made it so easy. He didn't make her feel bad for wanting him around.

Blythe: Fine. But don't go overboard.
   *Squirrel: Who, me? *wink**

Blythe rolled her eyes as she clicked off the phone and put it in her back pocket. One thing she'd learned about Sawyer was that he frequently went overboard. Why buy one bottle of detergent when they were on sale? He'd buy three. If she said she liked something, the next day she'd have half a dozen of them. T-shirts, a type of fruit, bras. That last one had been surprising and a little embarrassing.

They'd been making out on the couch one night and she'd taken off her shirt. Sawyer had seemed fascinated with the bra she'd been wearing. It was one of the ones Beth had ordered for her. It wasn't anything fancy, but it was super comfortable, and when Sawyer had simply stared at her for a long minute, not saying a word, she'd felt awkward and blurted out that she loved the bra. It had been so long since she'd had a comfortable bra, she wore that particular one all the time.

He hadn't taken her bra off. They'd made out and he'd put his hands on her, but they hadn't gone any further. She couldn't be upset with him though because the way he'd looked at her made her feel more beautiful and desired than she ever had before.

Three days later, a package arrived with a dozen more of the exact same brand and style of bra. All cotton. In all different colors. When she'd complained, Sawyer had simply shrugged. "You like them. They're comfortable. And now you have one in every color so you can wear it no matter what outfit you choose."

It was sweet and exasperating all at the same time. She'd learned to keep her enthusiasm to a minimum when she was around him. He'd spoil her rotten in no time if she let him.

Blythe did her best to make sure Sawyer knew how much she enjoyed being with him, as well. One night, they'd gone out with some of his firefighter friends, and when other women began to eyeball him, she was happy to let them know Sawyer was off the market. She'd put her arm around his waist and leaned into him, pleased when he didn't stop the conversation he was having with Driftwood, but simply put his arm around her shoulders in return.

If she was being honest, she knew that while she wanted to let Sawyer know she liked hanging out with him and being with him, she was actually reassuring herself at the same time. Hell, Sawyer probably hadn't even noticed the other women staring because he didn't think anyone looked twice at him when he was around his friends...which was ridiculous.

Making sure the women at the nearby table who were eye-fucking her man saw, Blythe had put her hand on his chest as she'd leaned in and whispered in his ear. All she asked was if he wanted another drink, but when he turned and kissed her on the forehead and told her he was good, Blythe was thrilled, and not only because it clearly communicated to the other women that he was hers. She also liked the easy way he touched her and the way he didn't care about being affectionate in public, and in front of his friends. His casual affection went a long way toward making her understand he was truly serious about wanting to be with her. That he wasn't embarrassed about her background.

As she walked back to the house, Blythe's phone rang. She pulled it out and saw that Beth was calling.

"Hey, Beth."

"Hi, Blythe. So...I did some digging into your financial background, like you asked me to."

"And?" Blythe's stomach cramped, and she stopped in the middle of the sidewalk and put a hand on her tummy to try to control the way it dipped and swirled, threatening to make her throw up right there.

"You owe a crap-ton of money."

Blythe couldn't stop the snort. "No shit."

"Yeah, I didn't think that would be a surprise."

"It's not." Blythe sighed. "I guess I'll be living off of other people's charity for a long time, huh? There's no way I can pay that kind of debt back in this lifetime."

"Bankruptcy," Beth said.

"What?"

"You need to declare bankruptcy. It's not ideal, I get that. But, girl, you have nothing to lose. Many people don't want to do it when they have huge bills because they have investment accounts, and when you declare bankruptcy, they take almost everything. But you have nothing. And I searched. No long-lost relatives who left you money you don't know about, no secret stash of money left by your mom. You're flat broke."

Blythe couldn't help but smile. She liked Beth. She told it like it was. "True."

"Now, there are some drawbacks…like it'll be on your credit report for seven to ten years, but once it's done, you don't have to worry about the medical bills or credit card debt hanging over your head anymore."

"I have no idea where to start."

"That's why you have me. And Soph. And Adeline and all the others. We'll figure it out and get you through it. Together."

Blythe looked up at the sky and took a deep breath. It had been so long since she'd been able to truly take in her surroundings. When your stomach was cramping because you were hungry and you smelled like fermenting trash, it was hard to appreciate any beauty around you.

But as Blythe fought to keep the tears from falling, she saw how big and fluffy the clouds looked. The sky was a beautiful light blue, and a memory of her and her mom lying on the grass in a park near their apartment when she was little, flitted through her brain. She'd forgotten a lot of the good times with her mom, the sad memories overtaking them. No more. Blythe made a mental vow to consciously pull the happy memories out of her brain and share them with her friends.

"Blythe? You still there?" Beth asked.

"Yeah, I'm here. And thanks. Seriously. I have no

idea how I got so lucky, but I sometimes feel as if I'm Alice and I've woken up on the other side of the looking glass."

Beth laughed at her analogy. "Whatever."

"Oh, and I got a job today. And I'm buying you and everyone else a drink with my first paycheck. I'm going to blow it all on my new friends. You had better be there."

"Only if Second gets a bone out of it," Beth quipped.

"The biggest one I can find," Blythe swore.

"You're good people," Beth said softly. "I've been where you are. Not exactly, but needing friends at a low point in my life. I didn't think anyone could ever look past my issues and see *me*. But Cade did. And the others. I'm just returning the favor. I'll talk to you later."

Beth hung up without another word, but Blythe couldn't be upset with her. She'd heard how emotional the other woman was. It was hard to admit that you needed help. And Blythe hadn't even really needed to admit it. The others just knew. Yes, she'd asked Beth to see what she could find out about the hospital bills and the other creditors she owed money to, but she'd gone further and come up with a solution.

Blythe figured sooner or later, she would've realized on her own that declaring bankruptcy was the best way to go, but it helped to have someone who wasn't directly affected taking a look at the situation.

Blythe resumed walking toward her house, feeling a hundred pounds lighter. All her problems weren't solved. She still didn't really have much that was hers and hers alone. But she had a job and a plan for her future. It would be a long haul, but she'd get there. She didn't need a huge house and a lot of stuff; her recent history assured her of that. She'd learned the most important thing was friends. People who would stand by you when you needed them.

Thinking about friends once again led to thoughts of Hope and her son, Billy. She hated that she hadn't been able to find them. Hated that they could still be on the streets right now.

She was on her way back to a normal life, but what about Hope? What about Billy? If someone like Dog or Tweek got their hands on him, they'd turn him into a little thug.

She suddenly felt guilty about living in Sophie's house. It wasn't huge, but it was more than adequate. Hell, she would've been happy with one room in the house. As long as she was safe from those who wanted to hurt her, she was good.

An idea came to her. It was crazy, but Sophie was so tenderhearted; Blythe knew without a doubt that she'd agree. Convincing Chief and probably Sawyer would be tougher.

Squaring her shoulders, Blythe continued toward home.

Home.

It wasn't, exactly. Yet for now, it was.

And hopefully, it would be for Hope and her son. And others after them.

Her thoughts turned to Sawyer. She'd never been to his place, but knew he owned his own house a couple miles from where she was currently living. He'd said it was similar to Sophie's house. Had four bedrooms, two bathrooms, a one-car garage, and a tiny yard. Sawyer admitted that he didn't like mowing and weed-eating, so it suited him just fine.

All of a sudden, Blythe really wanted to see it. Knew it would tell her a lot about the man she had come to care about a great deal.

She liked Sawyer. A lot. But more than that, she wanted him. She'd come to know him really well. All those months of texting and talking had laid the foundation for a really strong friendship. And being around him in person made that friendship grow into more.

She was attracted to him. It seemed like such a lame word. "Attracted." Screw that. Ever since he'd told her that he wanted to prove he could make her come more times than her high school chess club boyfriend, she'd fantasized about him doing just that. His mouth on her, his fingers, his intense gaze fixated on her. And she wanted to show him right back that whatever inadequacies he had about his own looks were totally unfounded...at least as far as she was concerned.

The more she was around him, the hotter he got. He was the total package.

Making a decision as she turned into her neighborhood, Blythe smiled. She'd already come such a long way from the scared, unsure woman who'd lived on the streets. The more she hung around the other firefighters' women, the more confident she got.

She wanted to see Sawyer's home, convince him to take her downtown and help her find Hope and Billy, and she needed him naked, inside her...not necessarily in that order.

Sawyer might want to celebrate her new job his way, but by the end of the night, she'd have her own celebration. With him in her bed. But this time, with both of them naked and satisfied after several orgasms.

She smiled the rest of the way home and plotted how to make it happen.

* * *

At five-thirty on the dot, Sawyer pulled up to the house. Blythe was ready and waiting for him when he stepped out of his Jeep and walked up to the door. She took a moment to appreciate his form as he came toward her.

He was tall, but not overly so. He was lean, but muscular at the same time. The tight dark blue polo shirt he wore highlighted his biceps. His stomach was flat and his jeans made his legs seem like they went on and on. He had on a pair of black boots, the ones he wore all the time, both to work and on his days off. He walked with a confidence that turned her on.

Blythe knew without a doubt that she was safe with him. He could handle any emergency that might come up. It had become second nature to constantly be on the lookout when she was walking around, but with Sawyer at her side, she didn't need to. If someone harassed them, he'd be there to put that person in their place. When they were in a store or restaurant, he kept his eyes peeled for anything that might put them…her…in danger. More than once, he'd gently steered her away from someone who came too close to her.

"Hey," she said when he stepped up on the porch.

"Hey," he returned. Without pausing, he kept coming toward her until he was in her space. One hand went around her waist and he pulled her to him. He leaned down and kissed her as if they were an old married couple.

She welcomed the kiss, wrapping her arms around his waist as he pulled back long enough to say, "Congratulations, baby. Proud of you."

There it was again. Hearing him say he was proud of her made butterflies swirl in her tummy. "Thanks. It's not a huge deal. It's only part-time and only minimum wage."

"I know, you said that before, but it doesn't matter. It's a job. It's the first step toward getting back to where you want to be."

"About that..." Blythe paused. She hadn't talked about this with anyone else. Hadn't even really thought much about what she wanted to do with her life until that afternoon, when she'd thought about Hope and Billy.

Sawyer didn't press her to talk, simply waited for her to get her thoughts together and talk to him on her own terms. It was one of a hundred and forty-three things she loved about him. He never rushed her. Never tried to pry into her mind.

"I don't want to go back to the factory to work."

"I don't blame you."

"I think I want to go back to school and finish my degree. I want to get into some sort of social work. I want to help people like me. Like my friends who are still out there on the streets."

Blythe held her breath, waiting to see what Sawyer thought. Her mom had been her biggest cheerleader, and she'd been disappointed yet proud of Blythe when she'd quit going to college to help take care of her. But it had been a long time since Blythe had truly cared about what someone else thought of her. And she cared what Sawyer thought. A lot. More than was probably normal for someone in her position.

"I think that's an amazing idea. They need people like you on the front lines. Someone who's been there. Someone who can really empathize, rather than just sympathize with the homeless."

"Really?"

"Really," Sawyer concluded firmly.

"I want to go see them," Blythe blurted. "Especially my friend Hope. She has a little boy, Billy. He..." She took a deep breath. They hadn't talked again about the night she'd called to tell him about Milena and her friend being kidnapped, but Blythe couldn't *not* think about it. "I told you Billy was abducted. That's why I had to tell that guy where

Milena was. I didn't want to, but he showed me a picture of Billy all tied up and scared."

Sawyer tightened his arms around her. "It's okay, baby."

Blythe shook her head. "It's not really, but if I had to do it again, I'd probably do the same thing. You should've seen Billy when I went and got him after that asshole told me where he was. He couldn't even talk to me, he was that scared. And Hope…she cried so hard when I brought Billy back to her. She feels awful for being homeless. Feels like she's failing her son. She even talked to me once about going back to her abusive ex-husband. Said being beaten every day almost seemed better than living with the dangers on the street."

Sawyer immediately shook his head. "No, she can't go back."

"I know. I told her the same thing. I need to find them," she said quietly. "It's been months. I need to make sure they're okay."

"I'll take you down there. I don't want you going by yourself. They could be anywhere," Sawyer told her.

"I'd like that."

"We'll go as soon as we can."

Blythe smiled at him. "Thank you. I didn't expect you to drop everything and go right away."

"They're your friends and you're worried about them. I'd be a dick to not take you down there as soon as possible."

"And...do you think..." Blythe bit her lip. This was harder.

Sawyer ran his hand over her short black hair and smiled tenderly at her. "Let me guess...if we find them, you want to bring them back here."

She sighed in relief. "Is that crazy? I mean, Sophie was nice enough to let Tadd and Louise stay here when they were recovering from that fire, and then she let *me* stay. I'm sure she has plans to sell the house at some point. Letting all of us refugees live here rent-free isn't exactly a sound business decision."

Sawyer leaned forward and rested his forehead against hers as he spoke. "Sophie is one of the nicest women I've ever met. She would no more kick you out than she would anyone who needed a helping hand. I'll run it by Chief to see what he thinks, if that would be okay."

Blythe nodded and buried her head into the space between Sawyer's shoulder and neck. "Thank you," she murmured into his skin. "Thank you so much. The house is definitely big enough, they could both easily stay here with me. And now that I'm working, I can help get food and stuff. There's a school down the block too, Billy can go to school and—"

"Move in with me," Sawyer said, pulling back and looking at her with such intensity, Blythe could only stare back at him in shock. "I know it's fast, but it doesn't feel fast to me. I've been sleeping over here for the last couple of weeks and when I'm at the station, I find myself missing you something awful. I like waking up with you in my arms. I like laughing with you and standing side by side with you in the kitchen as we make dinner."

"But...what if it doesn't work out? Where will I go?"

Sawyer's jaw ticked, but he didn't raise his voice or otherwise lash out at her. "I swear you will never end up on the streets again. I'm going to do everything in my power to make you want to stay with me. But if for some reason we decide that we can't cohabitate together, I'll make sure you have a place to go. Back here to Sophie's house or into an apartment. But regardless of our relationship, you will *never* sleep on the street again. You have my promise."

It sounded too good to be true, but then again, everything that had happened to her over the last month sounded that way. Blythe never would've thought she'd be assaulted then given a free place to stay. And now Sawyer. She wasn't an idiot. They'd been dancing around each other for weeks now. They were attracted to each other, and God only knew why they hadn't actually made love yet.

Besides, hours earlier, Blythe had been thinking about doing whatever she could to move along her relationship with Sawyer. This would certainly do it. Not only that, she *did* want to live with him. Wanted to wake up with him and go to sleep in his arms every night. Moving in with him would give Hope and Billy a chance at a more normal life.

"Okay," she said softly.

"Okay?" he repeated. "You'll move in with me?"

"Yeah. If Sophie agrees to let Hope and Billy move in here, I'll come and live with you."

The smile he bestowed on her was beautiful. He had a gleam in his eyes and she'd never seen him look happier. The fact that her agreeing to live with him did that, was humbling. "I can't contribute very much to rent," she told him honestly. "I'll do what I can in regards to food though. I'll clean and cook and do our laundry to help earn my keep."

"Fuck that. I'm an adult. I've been living on my own for a long time. I can clean my own shit and cook my own food. And I can certainly do my own laundry."

Blythe's spirits fell a bit at hearing that. "But then what will I do to repay you?"

The smile dropped from his face. "You don't have to *do* anything, baby. I want you to live with me because I want *you*. Not what you can do for me. I want to see your hair on my pillow in my bed. I want to see your smile when I come home from a shift. I want to know you're happy and healthy and loving life. We'll share whatever chores there are in the house; that's what couples do. No more talk of paying rent or earning your keep. Okay?"

"Are we a couple?" she asked.

"Hell yeah, we're a couple," Sawyer growled before his head lowered once more. He kissed her again, a kiss so long and deep, Blythe forgot where they were. All she could feel and smell was Sawyer. He made her feel womanly again. Human. She loved everything about him.

That thought brought her out of her lust-filled fog. She blinked up into Sawyer's chocolate-brown eyes.

She loved him. They hadn't even had sex yet, and she loved him.

It was crazy. Impossible. And right.

Hugging him tight, Blythe took deep breaths and tried to get herself together.

"Now that we have that settled, you ready to get

your party on?" Sawyer asked, his hand moving slowly up and down her spine as she clung to him.

Blythe chuckled and took a step away from him. "I guess so. What do you have planned?"

Sawyer grinned. "You'll just have to wait and see."

"You went overboard, didn't you?"

"Yup." The admission was immediate and said without a hint of remorse.

She shook her head at him, then turned to lock the door. She felt Sawyer behind her and as soon as she was done, his hand was on the small of her back and he was leading her to his Jeep.

Blythe couldn't stop smiling.

CHAPTER TWELVE

"Chuck E. Cheese's?" Blythe asked incredulously when they pulled into the parking lot.

Squirrel couldn't stop smiling. He was happier than he could remember being in a long time. Blythe had said she would move in with him. He was already thinking about things he could do to make his house more welcoming for her. He was a bachelor after all, and his house was a bit masculine.

"Yup," he told her, cutting off the engine. "I decided that instead of a stuffy formal dinner, it might be more fun to cut loose. Besides, it's been a long time since I've played Skee-Ball. I was once the neighborhood champion, I'll have you know."

"Oh, yeah?" Blythe said. "I'll have *you* know that I had the high score on the Skee-Ball machine in my neighborhood arcade for years. I think there's still a plaque with my name on it in that place."

Squirrel loved bantering with her. "Well, *I* was invited by the President of the United States to come to the White House and be awarded with the Presidential Order of Skee-Ball Champions."

She reached for his hand at the same time he reached for hers as they walked toward the door. "That's nothing. I was interviewed by Stephen King, who was going to write my biography. It was going to be called, *No One Can Beat Blythe Coopman When It Comes to Skee-Ball.*"

Squirrel threw back his head and laughed as he opened the door to the restaurant. "Okay, you win."

She beamed up at him as she stepped into the pizza place. Squirrel leaned down and said right into her ear, "But I'm still going to beat you."

Blythe shoved at him and he laughed, wrapping his arm around her waist. The noise in the restaurant was loud. There were children running around and the sounds of bells, dings, and whoop-whoops echoed around them. But it still seemed as if it was just the two of them.

Squirrel hadn't ever brought a date to the kids' restaurant, but it somehow seemed right for Blythe. She'd had too little fun in her life recently, and he knew without asking that she wouldn't be comfortable with him taking her to an expensive restaurant. Not with her homelessness being so recent.

He didn't particularly like the thought of her going back downtown to look for her friend, but he couldn't blame her for wanting to. If he'd gotten to know someone in the same situation as she'd been in, and if that friend had a young child, he'd do whatever it took to get them help.

Squirrel already knew Chief and Sophie wouldn't have an issue with Hope and Billy living in the house next door to them because he'd already had a discussion with Chief just the other day about that very thing. How they were considering forming an LLC to help offset the costs and provide a sort of halfway house for people who were trying to get back on their feet. Anyone chosen to live in the house would be vetted extremely well, with Beth doing the background checks and hunting for anything that might raise a red flag. No one with a history of drug abuse or a criminal record would be allowed to live in the house. They truly wanted to help people who'd found themselves without a place to live through no fault of their own.

Hope and Billy would be welcome, just as Tadd and Louise had been, and just as Blythe was.

"I hope you don't mind," he told her as they followed the hostess to a table toward the back of the restaurant, "but I invited a few friends to come help celebrate with us."

They turned a corner and the hostess gestured to one of the smaller rooms. It was probably used for private birthday parties or something, but it was perfect for what Squirrel had in mind. A fun dinner followed by an hour or so of playing the games.

What he didn't expect was for Blythe to come to a dead stop in the doorway, then abruptly turn around. He had a feeling she would've left altogether if he wasn't standing there and hadn't taken her in his arms.

Her head dropped to his chest and her hands gripped the material of his shirt at his arms as if her life depended on it.

"Blythe?" he asked.

"No."

"No what?"

"I can't do it."

"Do what?" Squirrel was confused. He raised his head and met the concerned gazes of his friends. He'd gone all out and called everyone in their inner circle, firefighters and cops alike. Sledge was there, but Beth had passed, saying she'd call Blythe later. Crash and Adeline and Coco were there. As was Sophie, Chief, Taco, Driftwood, Moose, and Penelope. Only a few of their law enforcement friends could come on such short notice, as some were on duty. But Dax and Mackenzie were there. Along with Quint, Corrie, TJ, Milena, and Calder. Squirrel didn't see anything that would alarm Blythe so much she'd want to leave.

"Milena's here. I can't face her," she whispered.

Squirrel mentally kicked his own ass. He knew Blythe felt guilty for what happened to the other woman, but he'd been too focused on doing something nice for Blythe to realize how hard it might be for her to face Milena. He took Blythe by the shoulders and pushed her back slightly so he could see her face.

"It's fine, Blythe. Wouldn't you rather get it over with than put it off? She doesn't blame you in the least for what happened. All the blame is on Jonathan and Jeremiah, as it should be."

Blythe's lip quivered, but she bit it in an effort to control her emotions.

"They're good people," he said softly. "Trust me. I would never do anything that would bring you pain. Give them a chance."

He watched as she closed her eyes and took a deep breath. When she spoke, her voice was tentative and unsure. "Okay, but if I make a fool out of myself and ruin the celebration you planned, don't blame me."

Squirrel kissed her on the forehead and gave her a quick hug. "You won't ruin anything, and there's no backing out of our Skee-Ball showdown. Now, come on, let me introduce you to the people you don't yet know. We'll sit next to Crash and Adeline, okay?"

Her smile was a bit wobbly, but she finally nodded. "Thanks."

"Anytime, baby."

She turned and they walked into the room. Squirrel saw the brave smile Blythe put on her face and it only endeared her to him more. She was trying because these were his friends. It meant a lot to him. More than she knew.

"Hey, everyone, thanks for coming," he told the group.

There were several greetings returned.

Squirrel held Blythe's hand as he took her around the table. She was gripping his so hard, he knew he'd have marks from her fingernails, but he didn't complain. Just held on tightly as he made the introductions and she was congratulated by their friends.

"This is Daxton Chambers and his girlfriend, Mackenzie. Dax is a Texas Ranger and I've known him for years."

"It's good to meet you," Blythe said politely.

"Same," Dax said in a deep voice.

"It's about time, is all I have to say," Mackenzie said with a smile. "I mean, I've been bugging Squirrel forever to get off his duff and find a woman. And you're beautiful, and you make such a lovely couple! I'm sure you're thrilled to get the job at the library. Truth be told, I'm a bit jealous, I mean...a library! You'll get first dibs on all the new books that come in!"

Blythe smiled. Squirrel inwardly sighed in relief. Mackenzie could outtalk anyone, but she meant well and her goodness came through loud and clear in her words.

"Thanks. I love to read, but haven't had the opportunity in a while, so I'm excited about the chance to borrow some books," Blythe told her politely.

"As you should be. And don't hesitate to contact me if you need anything. I know you have Squirrel and the others, but don't forget about me and the other cop girlfriends. We're here too. We all stick together."

"Th-Thanks," Blythe stammered, seemingly surprised at the offer.

Squirrel stepped over to the next couple. "And this is Quint and Corrie. Quint works for the San Antonio Police Department. He's been helping

Detective Nelson with the investigation on Dog and Tweek."

"Boy, those two are assholes," Quint said without filtering his words. "You're lucky to have gotten away with just a few scratches."

"They were a bit more than scratches," Squirrel growled, pissed off all over again when he thought about the knife wounds Blythe had suffered.

"Stop being so insensitive," the woman at Quint's side said as she slapped him on the arm. She turned in Blythe's direction and held out a hand. "Hi, I'm Corrie."

Blythe looked down at the hand, which was outstretched a bit too far to her right to have been offered to her. She looked up at Squirrel in confusion.

Squirrel took Blythe's hand in his and reached for Corrie's. He brought them together as he said, "Blythe, Corrie is blind, but that didn't stop her from escaping two thugs who'd abducted her and strolling off into the forest to wait for Quint here to come to her rescue."

Blythe smiled as she shook Corrie's hand. "Wow. That's a story I can't wait to hear. It's good to meet you."

"You too. And it wasn't quite as dramatic as Squirrel is making it sound."

"Yeah, it was," Quint countered.

"Whatever," Corrie muttered, but she snuggled into Quint's side.

The next introduction would be the hard one, but Squirrel didn't hesitate. As he'd told Blythe, better to get it over and done with rather than have it stretch out. "Blythe, this is TJ Rockwell, and you've met Milena Reinhart. TJ is a Highway Patrolman, and he used to be in the Army. In case you didn't know, Milena is a nurse. They've also brought their two-year-old son, JT."

Squirrel saw Blythe swallow hard, then hold her hand out to TJ. "It's nice to meet you."

"Ditto," the large man returned.

Then she turned to Milena. She didn't hold out her hand, instead rubbing it against the side of her jeans nervously. "It's good to see you again."

"You too. And please, I can tell you feel awkward, but you have absolutely nothing to worry about. What happened to me and Sadie wasn't your fault. That asshole was going to get his hands on us one way or another. And I heard you did it because another little boy was in danger?" Milena paused and looked at the chair next to her, where her son was frantically coloring outside the lines on the kids' placemat in front of him. She ran a hand over his blond hair and said softly, "I would've done the same thing."

"I'm so sorry," Blythe whispered. "I didn't know what else to do. I..." Her voice trailed off when Milena stood.

The other woman wrapped her arms around Blythe in a hug, and it was all Squirrel could do not to let out a huge sigh of relief. He hadn't thought Milena'd held a grudge against Blythe, but anything was possible.

"Don't apologize. You did what you thought was right. It's over and done and I don't have any hard feelings toward you. None. Okay?"

"Okay," Blythe told her.

"Hey, I thought this was supposed to be a celebration. Why all the sad faces?" Calder asked from next to them.

Squirrel slapped his friend on the back. Calder was a medical examiner who spent most of his time in the morgue and lab. He assisted law enforcement in investigations by giving his insights into how victims were killed.

"Blythe, this reprobate is Calder Stonewall. He's an ME with Bexar County and one of the smartest men I know."

"Nice to meet you," Blythe said as she held out her hand.

Calder shook it and winked at her. "Congrats on the new job. If there were more librarians who looked like you at the library when I grew up, I might have gone more often."

Squirrel rolled his eyes. "She's not a librarian," he told him. "And it's just a stepping stone to what she really wants to do."

"And what's that?" Calder asked.

Squirrel opened his mouth, then shut it at the last minute. He realized that he might be overstepping his bounds here. He turned to Blythe, only to see her eyeing him with amusement.

"You might as well tell him," she said. "Just pretend I'm not here."

"She's got you there!" Mackenzie hollered from down the table.

Squirrel knew he was blushing, but gamely continued. "She wants to get a degree in social work so she can help people in situations like she was in."

"That's amazing," Adeline chimed in. "I think it's great."

Blythe looked at Milena as she spoke. "There's this woman, her name is Hope, and she has a little boy. I don't know much about her situation, except that it involves an abusive ex, but I want to do more to help people like her. And her son. No one deserves to be on the streets, being treated like invisible second-class humans. I've been there. I want to help."

"What can we do to help Hope and her son?" Milena asked gently.

Blythe shrugged. "I was going to talk to Sophie about them," she admitted, looking over at the other woman.

"If you're going to ask if they can s-stay at the house, the answer is yes," Sophie said immediately. "But it m-might get a bit crowded."

"Blythe's going to move in with me," Squirrel informed his friends.

Everyone was silent for a second as his words sank in—then pandemonium broke out. The congratulations rang thick in the air and Squirrel could only smile at the genuine happiness his friends exuded. Many people might warn him that it was too soon, that he was making a mistake; that maybe Blythe, a former homeless woman, would rob him blind. But not his friends. They were happy for him. For *them*. It was no wonder he'd do anything for these people.

"Thanks," he said, holding his hands up to quiet everyone down. "Now...who's hungry? We have a celebration to start!"

And with that, everyone cheered and began talking amongst themselves once again.

Blythe turned to him and hugged him.

"Okay?" Squirrel asked quietly.

"More than," Blythe responded. She looked up at him. "I'm not saying that I'll never feel guilty again about what happened to Milena, but you were right, it was better to just get the meeting over with. She's really nice."

"Told you."

"So you did." Blythe smiled up at him. "I'm starving. What kind of pizza are we having? And will it come soon? I'm in the mood to kick a little Skee-Ball ass tonight."

Three hours later, Blythe was still laughing as Sawyer led her out of the restaurant and toward his Jeep. They'd played game after game of Skee-Ball, he'd won a few and she'd won a few. But more importantly, they'd had fun. A lot of fun. They'd laughed and good-naturedly exchanged quips all night.

She'd loved watching him with his friends, and JT. He'd patiently helped the toddler throw the ball down the lane and had clapped enthusiastically when he'd finally gotten it all the way and into one of the holes.

He'd talked her into playing a game of foosball with TJ and Milena, and they'd decided to play guys against girls. She was awkward around Milena at first, but the game was a great way of forging a bond. And they'd almost won too. If Sawyer hadn't cheated on the last goal he'd made, they would've.

Overall, Sawyer was hilariously funny. Not only that, but he stayed by her side for most of the night, making sure she was comfortable with everyone. Good-looking, hysterical, compassionate, giving, and sensitive. She couldn't believe he was hers.

Well, he wasn't officially hers yet, but she wanted him to be.

He pulled into her driveway and they both got out. He took her keys and opened the front door, holding out an arm for her to precede him. She walked in and put her purse on the small table in the foyer, then turned to him. "You're staying, right?"

"If you want me to," Sawyer said, putting his hands on her hips and pulling her into him.

"I want you to," she reassured him. Fingering the skin of his chest at the vee of his shirt, she said, "Thank you for tonight. I had a good time."

"Me too. You deserved to let loose and have a good time, baby."

She shrugged. "Maybe. Maybe not. It's not like I

got some awesome kick-ass job, but regardless, it was fun."

"Hey," he said, moving his hands to either side of her head and making her look at him. "It's a job. It's a step in the right direction. Yeah, maybe it's not your dream job, but it's something. I'm going to make sure I'm here to help you celebrate every little step forward. Life is too short to not smile, have fun, and gather with friends. Right?"

"Right," Blythe said softly. She reached up and grabbed his wrists with her hands. "Make love to me," Blythe blurted, then blushed hotly. She hadn't meant to just throw it out there like that, but she was burning up inside from want of him. They'd spent night after night snuggled close together, but she wanted more.

Without answering, Sawyer dropped his head. He kissed her as if his life depended on it. Blythe opened to him, giving him all of her without fighting. She'd give him whatever he wanted.

She felt him backing her down the hallway to the master bedroom. He never stopped kissing her and didn't move his hands from her face. She held on to his arms as they moved, trusting him as he moved her where he wanted her.

Feeling the bed at the back of her legs, Blythe sat, smiling when Sawyer followed her down. She shifted backward until she was lying crosswise on the bed. He finally lifted his head.

"Are you sure?"

"Positive."

"You won't regret this," he vowed.

"I know I won't. I want you, Sawyer. I want to fall asleep with your skin against mine. Your heartbeat at my back, your arms around me, keeping me safe. I want to know you...all of you."

"Fuck," Sawyer swore, then he was kissing her again, but this time it wasn't quite as controlled. His hands went to the hem of her shirt and pushed it upward, raising the material. The calluses on his hands lightly scratched the sensitive skin of her belly, and Blythe moaned into his mouth at the feel.

At the small sound, he pulled back and asked, "Okay?"

"More than," she reassured him. Then she arched her back and wiggled under him until she could get her shirt up and over her head. He was straddling her then, looking down at her as if she were made of fine silk instead of flesh and blood.

Deciding she wanted to hurry this along, Blythe reached behind her and unclasped the cotton bra she was wearing. She pulled it down her arms, trying not to blush. Once it was off, she reached for Sawyer's hands and placed them over her boobs.

"Touch me," she ordered. Then, hoping to goad him on and snap him out of whatever trance he'd fallen into, she said not so innocently, "You know, Ronald moved faster than you are right now."

* * *

Squirrel was terrified of doing something that would make Blythe change her mind. He would've backed off immediately if she'd decided that making love to him wasn't what she wanted after all, but he was silently praying she wouldn't come to her senses anytime soon.

He watched as she took off her shirt and couldn't wait to finally make her his. His cock was as hard as it had ever been and the only thing he could think of was getting inside Blythe and pounding into her so hard, she'd feel him for days.

Every morning, he jacked off in the shower to thoughts of how she'd feel around his dick. She'd be hot and tight…and he knew he'd blow the second he got inside of her.

When she undid her bra and put his hands on her silky flesh, Squirrel wanted to throw his head back and howl. Wanted to let everyone know she was his. That he'd never give her up.

He paused at the thought. He needed to calm down. Needed to make this good for her.

But he wasn't as sexually experienced as some. He'd had sex before, but the women had never mattered as much as Blythe.

All of Squirrel's old insecurities came rushing back to him—and he froze.

What was he doing? She was going to take one look at him without his clothes on and tell him to fuck off. His cock wasn't huge, it was just average... well, as far as he could tell. He'd always heard how much women liked big dicks. What if he couldn't satisfy her? What if she laughed when he took his pants off?

He was in the middle of a brewing panic attack and about to decide this wasn't going to work after all when she spoke.

"You know, Ronald moved faster than you are right now."

He stared down at her for a minute...then suddenly relaxed.

This was Blythe. She wasn't going to laugh at him. Wasn't going to think he was too small, too scrawny, too anything.

Even so, he'd just have to make sure she was limp with pleasure before he even took off his pants. And her reminding him that she liked nerdy guys was exactly the right thing to do, even if it annoyed him that she was bringing up an old lover when they were in bed.

"That boy might've moved faster, but I guarantee when tonight is done, you won't even remember that asshole's name."

And with that, Squirrel set about seducing his woman.

CHAPTER THIRTEEN

*B*lythe moaned when Sawyer leaned over and took one of her nipples into his mouth.

It felt amazing. Beyond amazing. Fucking phenomenal. Her breasts had never been that sensitive, but Sawyer's mouth and hands made her feel like a different person.

While his mouth was busy with one nipple, his fingers were playing with the other. She brought a hand up and pushed against the back of his head, encouraging him to suck harder. But instead of doing so, he lifted off her breast with a small pop and looked down at her. "You like that?"

"Sawyer," she whined. "Don't stop."

"You like that," he repeated in a smug tone.

"Of course I do," she said snarkily. "You're sucking on my nipple. What's not to like?"

He grinned at her and, keeping eye contact, leaned down again. He hadn't taken off his glasses and they'd slipped down his nose a bit. Watching him suck at her while his glasses barely hung on to his face was a huge turn-on for some reason. His tongue came out and he licked at her erect bud. Each pass of his tongue made her pussy contract. It was as if he had some sort of electric tongue or something.

Blythe groaned and closed her eyes.

She felt Sawyer shift and the weight of his body dropped down, his legs fitting between her. Over the next couple of minutes, Blythe could barely think...or move. His body weight held her down while his hands plumped and caressed her breasts. His mouth moved from one nipple to the other. Nipping, sucking, teasing.

"Please, Sawyer. More. I need more," she begged when it seemed like he would be content to suck on her breasts all night. She brought her feet up until they were flat on the bed next to his thighs. Then she relaxed her legs and let them fall open.

Without a word, Sawyer shifted until he was lying between them, his head level with her crotch. Her skirt had ridden up, and instead of pulling it off, he simply pushed it all the way up until the wispy material was gathered at her waist. Putting his hands on her thighs, he pushed her legs open even farther.

Then he blew her mind.

Leaving her panties in place, Sawyer leaned forward and ran his nose up and down the soaked gusset. Blythe groaned at the intimate gesture. She shifted, suddenly self-conscious. She could feel how wet she was, and since the panties she'd put on were a pale purple, she had a feeling he could *see* exactly how wet she was.

"Easy, baby," he murmured as if he knew she was embarrassed. Then he brought a hand up and traced her folds through the material. "This is so sexy. *You* are so sexy. I wish you could see this. Right here," he pressed against the fabric with his finger, "it's light purple. While here," he moved his finger and ran it down over her mons, "is darker. Is all this because of me?"

Blythe could only nod. No words would leave her mouth. She'd had no indication that Sawyer would be the type who liked to talk during sex. He seemed more like the strong-and-silent type. The kind of man who took what he wanted but didn't vocalize it. Seemed she was wrong.

"All this, just for me." Then he leaned down and licked over her folds. The feeling was muted because of the material between her skin and his tongue, but she still felt him.

"Fuck, you taste good," Sawyer murmured. Then he hooked the gusset of her panties with a finger and stretched it to the side. The cool air hitting her hot folds was a shock, but the second the sensation of coolness hit her, his tongue was there.

Arching into his mouth without thought, Blythe's hands went to his head and tried to grip his hair. Because it was so short, she didn't have anything to grab. Her fingernails dug into his scalp as she cried out.

Sawyer didn't seem to notice, or maybe he just didn't care. His tongue swiped from the bottom of her folds to the top. Then he did it again. And again. He didn't touch her clit, and Blythe squirmed in his grasp, needing him to touch her there.

She thought she heard him chuckle but was too aroused to return his smile.

Just when she was going to beg him to touch her clit, his tongue began to circle the taut bud. Blythe frantically shifted her hips, trying to get him to put more pressure where she needed it, but he refused to give in to what she wanted.

After a minute of the erotic torture, she broke.

"Please, Sawyer! Suck my clit. Stop teasing me. I

need—oooh!" Her words cut off when he did just as she begged.

Using the tip of his tongue, he licked right over her clit hard and fast.

Her hips came up off the bed as she pushed herself closer to his talented tongue. She felt a bead of sweat roll down her temple into her hair, but Blythe could only concentrate on one thing. Coming.

After ten seconds or so of Sawyer's direct attention on her clit, she exploded. The orgasm welling up from her belly and spreading throughout her body like wildfire. Her body no longer her own, Blythe's hips thrust upward, her thighs shook, and she panted for air as the pleasure consumed her.

Just as she was coming down from the euphoric high, she felt Sawyer's finger ease inside her soaked canal. Whimpering now, she could only feel as he caressed her inner walls. She wasn't sure what he was doing, but she didn't have the brain power to ask as he gently probed her sheath.

It felt good—but then he touched something that made her excitement ramp up several notches. "Sawyer!" she exclaimed as he touched it again.

"That's it," he murmured, and his finger more aggressively began to stroke her G-spot deep inside her body.

"Oh, fuck," Blythe exclaimed as her butt clenched and her thighs tensed. Another orgasm was fast approaching and there was nothing she could do to stop it. The intense feelings almost hurt. Almost.

The second Sawyer clamped his mouth around her clit and sucked hard, she came. It felt as if she was never going to stop. She clenched around the finger inside her and could only moan as her body went into overdrive. She vaguely heard Sawyer's groans of approval as he played her body like a violin.

Having no idea how much time had passed, Blythe came back to herself when she felt Sawyer's body weight leave her. Her eyes opened into slits and she watched as he tore his shirt up and over his head. His nipples were little points and she could see a patch of pink on his upper chest. As if what he'd done had aroused him just as much as it had her.

She had no idea what Sawyer was self-conscious about when it came to his body. He didn't have bulging muscles, but he was very clearly in shape. He had those defined vee muscles women seemed to go crazy over, pointing down to his crotch. The smattering of hair on his chest was sexy as hell and she loved how, when he moved, she could see his muscles tensing and flexing.

He was breathtaking—and she couldn't believe

he was all hers. She wanted to lick him from top to toe and reassure him that he had nothing to worry about in regards to his looks.

"Take your panties off," Sawyer ordered as he began to unbutton his jeans. She couldn't tear her eyes from between his legs. She couldn't wait to see his cock. She lifted her butt and yanked her underwear down her legs. He pulled down his pants and boxer briefs at the same time—and all Blythe could do was sigh when she saw how aroused he was.

Yeah, he'd definitely liked making her come, that was obvious.

His cock was hard and pointing toward her as if it knew exactly where it wanted to be. The head was a dark purple, and it actually looked painful. He wasn't super long, but he was thicker than anyone she'd had before. A shiver of excitement went through her.

Without a word, Sawyer palmed his cock and stroked it. He kept his eyes on hers...and suddenly, Blythe realized he was nervous.

"God, you're gorgeous," Blythe said softly. "I can't believe I've already had two of the most intense orgasms I've ever had and all I can think about is you getting inside me and doing it again."

"Fuck," Sawyer swore.

That one word said so much. It was filled with disbelief, wonder, and relief all at the same time.

"I'm not huge," he said, still lightly stroking his dick.

Blythe had been mesmerized by his hand, but at his words, her gaze shot up to his. "And my boobs aren't anything to write home about. I'm still too skinny, yet I've got too much junk in my trunk."

He growled at her and narrowed his eyes. "You're perfect. Don't put yourself down."

"And don't *you* put *yourself* down," she retorted. "I want you, Sawyer. Although now you've ruined my mellow post-orgasm mood. You want reassurances? Fine—I've never seen a more beautiful cock." She propped herself up on an elbow and reached out for him.

Pushing his hand away from his dick, she palmed his cock. Stroking up and down, she was amazed at how soft his skin was. He was rock hard under her caress, and she couldn't wait for him to get inside her.

Her voice lowered as she concentrated on his dick. "You're perfect, Sawyer. Seriously. Most women aren't into monster dicks. That shit hurts, you know? Besides, you've got the girth to compensate."

"Enough," he ordered, pushing her hand away

and squeezing the base of his dick so hard it had to have hurt. He put a hand in the middle of her chest and pushed.

Blythe obeyed and fell back. She lifted the edge of her skirt that had fallen back down over her lap and spread her legs wide and said, "Fuck me, Sawyer."

And just like that, her bossy man was back. He leaned over and snagged his pants off the floor, pulling out his wallet. He opened a condom with his teeth and rolled it over his cock. Then he crawled over her and stared.

Blythe couldn't read the emotions she saw in his eyes. Her hands grabbed his forearms and she caressed them up and down.

"Once I enter you, you're mine," he declared.

Blythe nodded. "Okay."

"I mean it," he warned.

Blythe's brows drew down. "And I said okay."

His lips quirked then and he seemed to relax. "You do it."

"Do what?"

"Put me inside you."

"With pleasure." Wanting to give him a little payback for making her so crazy and turned on, when Blythe reached between their bodies, she didn't immediately notch him to her opening; she ran her fingers up and down his rock-hard length.

"Stop teasing me and do it," Sawyer ordered.

Wrapping her hand around his cock, her fingers not even close to touching, she grinned. He *was* thicker than anyone she'd been with before. The thought aroused her more, even as it slightly concerned her.

She opened her legs as wide as she could and said softly, "Go slow. It's been a while for me, and you're a lot thicker than my old vibrator."

Sawyer groaned at her words. "Fuck, baby. You can't say shit like that right before I get inside you for the first time. I'm on a hair trigger as it is. Did you fuck yourself in this bed while I was sleeping out on the couch?"

She wanted to tease him more. To say yes, but she had to be honest. "No. But not because I didn't want to. One, I don't have a vibrator anymore. It's not like I could break it out in the middle of the sleeping room at the shelter. And two, even if I did have one, I probably wouldn't have used it because I would've been embarrassed if you heard it."

Sawyer began to slowly push inside her, even as he spoke. "I'm gonna get you one. I want to watch you fuck yourself with it. And don't ever be embarrassed about your sexuality, Blythe. It's a part of human nature. We all need it."

Blythe looked up at him with wide eyes. The

head of his cock was inside her now but he wasn't giving her any more of himself just yet. Even that much felt too big. Her hands tightened on his biceps as she stared up at him.

"Relax, baby. I got you."

He did. She knew that. She forced herself to relax all her muscles and when she did, his cock pushed inside her another inch or so.

They both moaned.

Sawyer braced himself on the mattress again. "Here we go," he warned—and then his hips moved.

Squirrel hadn't ever felt anything as amazing as being inside Blythe's body. She was soaked from the G-spot orgasm he'd given her. She was also tight. Extremely tight. He didn't know how long it had been since she'd had a cock inside of her, but he felt so honored that she was inviting *him* into her body.

The look on her face as she'd stroked him had erased years of feeling inadequate when it came to his dick. And when she'd started listing off the things about her body that she felt weren't attractive, he got it. Blythe didn't care about how big his dick was, or thick, or even about his looks. She enjoyed his body, she'd made that clear, but it was that she enjoyed what he *did* with his equipment. How he acted. How he treated her.

"Here we go," he warned Blythe, seconds before he sank balls deep inside her.

He saw her flinch slightly and held himself still. He could feel the material of her skirt pressed against his belly and it only made the moment more erotic. He hadn't bothered to undress her all the way before losing control and needing to get inside her body.

He stayed stock still, feeling every throb of the blood in his cock as his heart beat overtime. She was strangling his dick, and he wished for a second that he was bare inside her. That he could feel how wet she was on his skin. But then he shook his head. There would be time for that. This was about her, not him.

Squirrel knew he was about two seconds away from coming, but he held off. He still had to make her come three more times before the night was over. There was no way the faceless Ronald would one-up him. No fucking way.

When he felt Blythe's thighs relax around him, and when she was no longer digging her fingernails into his skin, he slowly sat back, pulling her hips with him as he did so. He was now sitting back on his heels and she was lying on her back, straddling his lap. He was still inside her, his cock twitching with every move. He wanted nothing more than to pump inside her, hard, but she needed to be mindless with pleasure before he did so.

"What are you—"

Blythe's question abruptly cut off when his thumb landed on her clit and he began to caress her roughly. He didn't let up as she squeaked, and he didn't stop when her hips tried to pull away from him.

His free hand gathered the material of her skirt and bunched it together on her stomach. He held her down as he continued his all-out assault on her extremely sensitive bundle of nerves.

"Sawyer!" she exclaimed as her hands gripped the sheet above her head.

"If I'm going to make you forget what's-his-name, you need to come three more times."

"I can't," she wailed, even as her body belied her words.

Squirrel was beginning to recognize the signs of her impending orgasm. He studied the woman writhing on his dick and memorized every nuance of her response. When he pressed directly on her clit, she slightly pulled away from him, but when he rubbed around it in circles, her hips raised, seeking more. Her chest was a rosy hue and her nipples were hard as nails on her chest. The closer she came to orgasm, the more she arched her back, the more her thighs shook, and the harder her inner muscles squeezed his cock.

It was the latter that almost did him in.

Letting go of her skirt, but not stopping his ministrations to her clit, Squirrel reached between them and grabbed hold of the base of his dick to try to hold off his own orgasm.

As his fingers brushed her sensitive inner thighs and the folds of her pussy, she exploded. Her hips, no longer held down by his hand, shot up, and he could feel every muscle in her body tighten. Remarkably, he also felt her sheath grow hotter and slicker from the juices her body produced.

"God, you're amazing," Squirrel breathed as the orgasm continued. Knowing she would be extremely sensitive, he took his finger off her clit, allowing her to start to recover. As soon as her eyes opened and she looked up at him, he moved. His thumb went back to her clit and his other hand went to her tits. He squeezed and pinched her nipples even as he swirled his thumb over her clit.

"God, no more, Sawyer. Please. I'm too sensitive. Ooooh, fuck…"

And that was that. She was so primed, she went off again in a less-intense orgasm. Her thighs were shaking nonstop now and he could feel every twitch of her inner muscles as her body went into overload.

He'd never been so aggressive with a woman before Blythe. Oh, he'd cared if his partners got off in the past, but nothing like this. It was a heady feeling, knowing he'd done this to her.

Squirrel held her hips to him as he moved, so as not to let his cock slip out of her. When her ass was back on the bed, he reached over and grabbed a pillow, shoving it under her hips.

Now her pelvis was tipped slightly upward, giving him exactly the right angle to take her. And he did just that.

Without easing into it, Squirrel pulled his dick out of her and slammed it back inside. They both moaned, and he did it again. Then again. He couldn't stop. She felt too good. So fucking hot.

She was wet, *very* wet. *He'd* done that. He'd made her gush with excitement and that was sexier than anything she could've said or done.

He would've worried he was hurting her, except when he glanced down at her face, she was smiling in a dreamy way that made his cock twitch even as it tunneled in and out of her pussy.

Looking between her legs as he thrust, Squirrel couldn't help but groan at the sight of his cock, covered in her juices, emerging from and disappearing into her folds. Her legs were splayed open bonelessly and he could see her body stretching around his girth. She seemed so small, but she took him perfectly.

It was that thought that pushed him over the edge. Squirrel thrust inside her once more and held himself as far inside her body as he could while he came. And came and came and came. He didn't think he'd ever come so hard or as much as he did when he was inside Blythe. He felt lightheaded as his orgasm continued on and on.

When he finally felt his cock stop twitching, he pulled out without a word and shifted onto his back. He pulled Blythe with him and she ended up straddling his chest. Squirrel palmed her ass and pulled her higher, toward his face. "Come up here, baby."

"Sawyer, no," she protested.

But he didn't give her any choice. He manhandled her until her folds were above his mouth. They were pink and slightly inflamed—and Squirrel couldn't wait to taste her once more.

He lifted his head and stuck his tongue inside her body as far as he could.

She jerked in his hold, then relaxed and moaned. He smiled.

Fuck, he loved eating her out. He'd always enjoyed oral sex, but Blythe's taste turned him on more than anyone he'd ever been with. She was tangy and slightly salty and he wanted that taste on his tongue for the rest of his life.

He didn't give her a chance to be embarrassed about what he was doing. Squirrel ate at her like he was a starving man who hadn't eaten in days. The juices from her previous orgasms dripped out of her like a faucet and he licked up every one.

In moments, his face was covered with her essence as she gyrated and moved above him. He moved one hand and lightly fingered the sensitive nerves around her ass as he ate her.

"Sawyer...oh my God...what are you...fuck...I'm going to come again!"

Her words were disjointed and music to his ears. Squirrel moved up to her clit and sucked hard even as his fingertip sank inside her still sensitive body. And just like that, she came again.

Squirrel couldn't stop smiling as he gently licked the new fluid that came forth as a result of her orgasm. Blythe was shaking above him and he carefully pushed her backward, away from his face, and pulled her down on top of him.

She fell as if she couldn't hold herself up, her legs dropping, one to either side of his. She lay sprawled on him, and he could feel her heartbeat strong and frantic against his own chest.

He didn't move for several minutes, letting her come down from her orgasmic high and enjoying the feel of her in his arms. This was what it felt like to truly be intimate with someone. He'd had sex, but he'd never been intimate. There was a big difference. The fact that Blythe wanted to be here with him changed his life.

"You win," Blythe muttered, her warm breath wafting over his chest as she spoke.

"Damn straight," Squirrel told her, knowing exactly what she was talking about. "Five. Dumbass chess boy has nothing on me."

Blythe chuckled. Then laughed. Then flat-out guffawed as his words sank in. He didn't laugh with her, just enjoyed the way her body moved against his as she laughed.

"I think I like the fact that you're so competitive," she said when she finally had herself under control.

"Good. I have a feeling I'll be needing to prove myself to you a lot in the future," Squirrel told her.

Her hand came up and rested against his chest. She slid off to his side and sighed in contentment. "You're amazing, Sawyer. And not just because you made me come five times. I've never…it's just…that was…"

"I know, baby. Shhhh, you don't have to talk."

"Thank you. I wondered if I'd ever feel sexual

ever again. After being on the streets, you kinda lose your own sense of self. Everything is about where you're going to find food, where you're going to sleep, and sex is the last thing you're thinking about...except for the fear of being raped, which is always in the back of your mind."

Squirrel's arms tightened around her at her words. He didn't like thinking about her being scared of being violated on top of everything else.

"But you just made me feel more like a woman than I ever have before. Thank you."

"It was my pleasure, baby."

"Was it?" She raised her head to look at him.

Squirrel eyed her incredulously. "Are you serious?"

She nodded.

"I've never come so hard in my life. I've never been so desperate to be inside a woman as I was with you. Then when I got in there, all I could think of was making it good for you. But yeah, it was amazing. Awesome. Awe-inspiring. Can we do it again?"

She smiled at him then. Her hand went down his body to his cock. "First you have to get it up— Shit, Sawyer! You're already hard again?"

He chuckled at the sound of awe in her tone. "Around you, I think it's a permanent condition." He caught her hand in his and brought it up to his mouth. He kissed the palm then held it to his chest gently. "You're exhausted and in no condition to go again just yet."

"You can say that again," she muttered.

"Come on," Squirrel said as he sat up, taking her with him.

She protested with a huge groan.

"You need to take off that skirt, as much as I love it, and I need to take care of this condom and clean up."

"Okay," she grumbled, but he saw her steal a glance between his legs.

He couldn't stop the words that popped out. "You're really okay with my size?"

Blythe looked at him then. She got up on shaky knees and Squirrel held her steady with his hands at her hips. "I'm really okay with everything about you, Sawyer. You fit me perfectly. And I think you know how well you pleased me. Drop it, yeah?"

"Yeah," Squirrel said, and he tried to tamp down the emotion threatening to bring him to his knees. If he'd known all those months ago when he'd given her his sweatshirt that she would make his life complete, he never would've let her evade him for so long.

He stood and went into the bathroom to clean up. As if her words were all the reassurance he'd needed, Squirrel strode back into the bedroom naked as the day he was born, and he didn't feel self-conscious about it for the first time in his life. How could he when Blythe's heavy-lidded eyes were glued to him as he moved?

She liked what she saw. Just as he liked what he saw as he came toward her. She'd removed her skirt and it was lying in a heap on the floor next to the bed. Her legs were slightly parted and her arms were thrown up over her head.

She looked exactly like a cover model—and she was all his.

Squirrel lay down on the bed and pulled her into his arms. She came willingly, hiking up one leg to rest on his thigh.

They didn't say a word as they cuddled. Eventually, Squirrel felt her breaths even out and knew the second she fell asleep. Her body got heavy against his as her muscles relaxed.

He smiled. He hadn't lied to her earlier. Now that he'd been inside her, she was his. He'd move heaven and earth to give her whatever she wanted and anything she needed. No matter what it was.

He had a wonderful family, and he'd known love. But he'd had no idea *this* kind of love existed. The kind where you would literally give anything and do anything to make sure the other person was happy and safe.

Sleep came quickly to him after that. Squirrel fell asleep with a smile on his lips and his arms tightly around the woman at his side.

CHAPTER FOURTEEN

*B*lythe eyed Sawyer's house with interest
as they pulled into his driveway. It was
bigger than she would've thought. He'd told her on
the way over that he'd gotten the four-bedroom,
two-bath house because of his sisters. They sometimes came over and spent the night and he wanted
to make sure he always had room for them.

The sentiment made Blythe feel a little weepy.
She'd longed for a sibling to share the responsibility
of caring for her mom. It made her feel guilty every
time she thought it, but even if she'd just had
someone to talk to, who could be a support system,
it would've made dealing with her mom's sickness
easier.

But it was the bone-deep conviction that if Charlotte, Natalie, or Emma ever needed a place to stay,

they had one with Sawyer, that made her almost lose it. Even sleeping on a friend's couch would've been better than what had happened to her. But she hadn't had anyone to ask. All her so-called friends had seemed to disappear into thin air after she'd had to stay home with her mom.

She and Sawyer had collected the things she'd been given since she'd moved into Sophie's house and packed them into his Jeep. It actually was going to take two trips to get everything moved, which surprised Blythe. She hadn't realized she'd accumulated so much stuff in such a short period of time. But she supposed that's what happened when you had extremely generous friends.

She'd made Sawyer wait until the following weekend to move her into his house because she'd wanted to finish her first week at the library and make sure the job really was going to work out. And it was. She loved the head librarian and everyone she'd met had been extremely nice.

"What are you thinking about so hard over there?" Sawyer asked as he waited for the garage door to go up.

"It's beautiful. Your house, I mean."

"Thanks. Still needs some work done here and there, but overall I'm pleased with it."

He shut off the engine after he'd pulled into the

garage and waited for her at the front of the Jeep. "We'll come back out and get your stuff after the tour. Okay?"

"Perfect. I can't wait to see everything."

He shrugged a little self-consciously. "Don't set your expectations too high. It's just a house."

Blythe turned to him and put her hands on his chest. They were almost eye to eye. "It's never *just* a house. Especially not to someone like me, who didn't *have* a home for a while."

"I didn't mean it like that. It's just...it's not fancy. I'm not the cleanest person around. I did my laundry, but I can't remember if I did the dishes this morning and there's probably a shit-ton of my stuff lying around that I haven't bothered to put away."

"All that means is that it's lived in. Seriously, Sawyer, stop worrying. Hell, you've spent most of your time at Sophie's house with me. Of course you haven't had time to clean up."

When the worried look didn't leave his face, she realized that he really was anxious about what she would think of his home. "Sawyer, not too long ago, I carried everything I owned on my back. I slept on the street in filth and disgusting stuff I couldn't even name. Your house isn't going to make me go running out into the yard, begging to be brought back to Sophie's. Trust me."

She could've sworn Sawyer blushed, but he dipped his head before she could be sure.

"I'm sorry. You're right. I just didn't want you to think you were about to walk into a staged home or something."

"No, I'm about to walk into *your* home. A home I feel blessed to have been invited into."

He lifted his head, a look of profound relief on his face, and nodded. "Okay, then let's do this. We need to go and get the rest of your stuff. I know we already went downtown and looked for Hope and Billy once, and you want to try again, but are you sure you won't let me go myself this time and see if I can find them for you?"

She shook her head. "No. I want to go and see the people I befriended. Some of the workers at the shelter are probably worried about me too."

They'd had this argument before, and she'd replied the same way every time he'd asked if she would let him go by himself. He was worried about Dog and Tweek finding her and doing something stupid. Blythe couldn't say she wasn't worried about that herself, but she wasn't going to let the two thugs keep her away from the people she knew and liked. Besides, Sawyer would be with her. He'd keep her safe.

Her mind went back to the couple she'd seen that

fateful night. She knew without a doubt that if it had been her and Sawyer that night, he would've done the same thing the other man had done. He would've put himself between her and Dog and Tweek, and made sure she didn't get hurt in any altercation.

Sawyer sighed and turned to the door. He grabbed her hand in his before he reached for the handle.

Blythe followed him inside and didn't say much as he led her from room to room. His kitchen counters and cabinets were a little outdated, but the stainless-steel appliances almost made her mouth water. Once upon a time, she'd liked to cook, and the sight of the sleek double convection oven and the gas drop-in stove made her want to whip up something for Sawyer.

He had a huge leather couch, which wrapped around one corner of the big living area, and an enormous flat-screen TV hanging on the opposite wall. He was right, there were knick-knacks strewn here and there. Books, shoes, even a T-shirt sitting in a lump on the floor, but it wasn't as bad as he'd made it out to be. The room simply looked lived in. Comfortable.

Sawyer pointed out the half bath and then went down a hallway to a workout room of sorts. There was a bench press and a bunch of free weights on the floor. There was also a treadmill in the corner.

He shrugged. "I might not be as strong or as big as my friends, but I still gotta work out to keep in shape."

Blythe couldn't help but smile. She used her free hand to run it up and down his arm. "Oh, you're in shape all right," she purred.

Sawyer merely rolled his eyes at her and shook his head. "Come on, woman. There's more to see."

"The bedrooms, I hope," she said with a lift of her brows.

Sawyer laughed out loud at that. "Oh yeah, baby. Lots of bedrooms to see." He then took her out of the small room and they went back to the living area. They went up a set of stairs to the second floor, where he quickly showed her two bedrooms that were relatively clean. "These are the rooms my sisters use when they're here."

He went by another door, and Blythe stopped him and gestured to it. "What's in there?"

"Another bedroom," Sawyer told her—without meeting her eyes.

"Ooooh, is this like the red room of pain?"

"What? I have no idea what you're talking about."

"You know, like in *Fifty Shades*."

Sawyer shrugged.

"The book?" Blythe pushed. "It was a huge hit, and then there was a movie made out of it."

"I'm guessing, from the sounds of it, it's a romance, right?"

She nodded.

"Do I look like the kind of guy who reads romance?"

"No, but looks can be deceiving. I know a lot of husbands and boyfriends read the book to get some tips."

Sawyer backed her against the wall right there in the hallway. "You think I need some tips, baby? You didn't think so last night when you were impaled on my cock and riding me like a professional cowgirl."

Blythe blushed. She *had* done that. But only after his encouragement and when he'd refused to push her over the edge of her orgasm. He'd told her that he wanted to see if she could make herself come while riding his dick, and without using her fingers. And she had. In spectacular fashion. "Okay, you win. You don't need to read romance or need any tips."

"Thank you," was his smug response.

"But I still can't believe you don't know about *Fifty Shades of Grey.*"

He began to pull her past the door once more, but Blythe resisted. "Seriously, Sawyer. What's in there?"

He sighed and dropped her hand. "It's silly. Go on, take a look."

Blythe didn't know why he was so uncomfortable, but now all sorts of awful things were going through her head. What in the world could be so embarrassing for him? She cracked open the door —and stared at the space in front of her in confusion.

Turning to him, she said, "I don't understand."

"The people I bought the house from were selling because they were moving to Montana to be closer to their family. They had two kids already, and the woman had been pregnant with their third. They'd decorated this room for their baby...but she miscarried. I couldn't bring myself to paint over the mural on the wall."

Blythe studied the room carefully. Noah's Ark had been painstakingly painted on the largest wall. There were pairs of lions, tigers, dogs, cats, birds, elephants, giraffes, and even a pair of sloths in a tree. The rest of the room was empty. Not one piece of furniture was in there. She turned to look back at Sawyer.

"I just...I thought it would be a perfect room for a child someday. It's stupid, I know. A bachelor keeping a room for a baby when he had no prospects on the table. But I just couldn't bring myself to make this into a guest room. It feels as if it's just waiting for a baby to occupy it."

Blythe was moved beyond words. Her man had so much more depth than he ever showed the world. She brought his hand up to her mouth and kissed his palm like he did to her all the time. Then she curled his fingers into his palm where she'd kissed him and held his hand in both of hers. "I agree. This room is perfect for a baby."

He wouldn't meet her eyes for the longest time, then finally took a deep breath and looked at her. "Last night I had a dream. And I swear to God I'm not making this up…"

When he didn't say anything else, Blythe prompted, "Yeah? A dream?"

"Yeah. I think I was nervous about you moving in and that's what caused the dream. But I was in this room, and it was fully furnished. A crib under the mural, a changing table near the window, a dresser over there." He pointed to the other side of the room without looking. "And a rocking chair. I was sitting in the chair, waiting for you. You walked into the room with something in your arms, and you came straight to me and leaned over and put it in mine. I remember being confused, but I didn't question you. I looked down at what you'd given me, and it was a baby. A tiny little baby boy. He was looking up at me with these huge hazel eyes, exactly like yours, and he smiled."

Blythe could barely breathe. All she could think about was the fact that the man she loved had dreamed about her giving him a baby.

Without thought, she dropped his hand and threw her arms around his neck.

They kissed as if this was the last day of their lives. The desperation and passion behind their kiss was something Blythe had never felt before. Oh, she'd been aroused with Sawyer, no doubt about it, but this was different.

She couldn't get close enough to him. Couldn't get enough of his hands on her body. Without stopping their kiss, she brought her hands to his pants. He did the same with hers. They fumbled with the buttons and zippers for a long moment as their mouths stayed fused together. Without a word, Sawyer gently pushed Blythe to the floor. He shoved her pants and underwear down just far enough so he could get his fingers inside her.

He roughly rubbed her clit, bringing her to the edge of climax within seconds.

"Sawyer," she moaned.

"Blythe," he returned, and moved his hand from between her legs to his cock. He notched the tip of his rock-hard dick to her folds and ordered, "Tell me yes."

"Yes. God, yes," Blythe moaned as she spread her legs as far as they could go with her pants still around her thighs.

He slowly pushed inside her, feeling that much thicker because she couldn't move her legs very far apart. Sawyer held her gaze as he thrust. The longer he pumped inside her, the wetter she got, until she knew she would leave a wet spot on the carpet under her ass.

"Love you," Sawyer said as he sank inside her. "Love you so fucking much."

"Sawyer!" Blythe gasped as he bottomed out inside her.

Then words were beyond both of them. Blythe felt the orgasm welling up inside her faster than ever before, and she grunted with each of Sawyer's thrusts. He was being more forceful than earlier, and she loved it.

They were both still wearing their shirts, shoes, socks, and most of their pants. The only skin she could feel of Sawyer's was his cock inside her. She hadn't meant to say them, but the words welled up from her soul and she couldn't hold them back anymore.

"I love you, Sawyer. So much!"

She saw his jaw clench, and his eyes glittered behind the lenses of his glasses. She erupted in a monster orgasm, and the way her body tightened must have pushed him over the edge as well. He shoved himself inside her once more and stayed there, his eyes never leaving hers as he filled her body with his come.

She realized they hadn't used protection the second she felt the warmth of his come fill her, but at the moment, she didn't care.

If it hadn't been for her clothes, Blythe knew she would've had rug burn on her shoulders, ass, and thighs. They'd fucked like animals in the middle of an empty room meant for a baby. She could barely wrap her mind around what had just happened.

"Fuck me," Sawyer groaned, then he finally closed his eyes and rested his forehead on hers.

"I just did," Blythe quipped, feeling amused more than panicked at what they'd done.

His eyes opened and he lifted his head. "I love you," he said softly, looking her right in the eyes as he said it.

"I love you too," Blythe echoed.

"I didn't mean to do this here."

Blythe chuckled. "I figured."

"Not that I don't always want to make love with you, but I told myself I was going to show you the house, get your stuff moved in, go back to Sophie's and get the rest of your stuff and bring *that* over. Then I was going to make you a nice meal. *Then* I was going to fuck your brains out. In my bed. Where you belong."

She melted at his words. "We can still do all that."

"Damn straight," Sawyer mumbled. Then sighed. "I didn't mean to do it without protection either." He gestured to their hips, which were still connected. He was still semi-hard inside her.

"It's okay."

"It's not. But you should know, I'm clean. I'd never put you at risk like that."

"I didn't even think about that," Blythe said. "I am too. I told you that you're the first guy I've been with in years."

"What about…you know?" he asked.

Blythe couldn't help but be amused. Sawyer was thirty years old and he still couldn't say the words. But her amusement didn't last long as she thought about his question. She shrugged. "I'm not on anything. Couldn't afford it and there wasn't a reason for it."

She watched, fascinated, as Sawyer took a deep breath. She could feel his cock twitch inside her as whatever he was thinking flickered through his brain and worked its way down to his cock.

"I love you," he repeated.

She could only nod.

"You getting pregnant wouldn't be the end of the world."

Holy shit. Had he really said that?

"Okay," she managed to say, still processing.

"Your mouth is saying okay, but your eyes are saying something completely different," he commented.

"Can we get up and talk about this?"

"No," he said immediately. "Talk to me, baby."

Blythe sighed and closed her eyes. She felt his fingertips running through her short hair, but he was giving her time to think. Finally, she opened her eyes to see his beautiful brown gaze looking worried.

"It's hard for me to think about having a baby right now. I've barely gotten off the street. I don't have any savings, I'm about to declare bankruptcy, I'm making minimum wage at a part-time job. I can't support myself. How in the world can I even *think* about bringing a baby into this life?"

"Because you're not alone anymore," was Sawyer's immediate response. "You've got me. And Sophie. And Penelope and Moose. And my family. And all the others. And I don't give a shit if you ever work again. I make good money. I'll never be a billionaire, but I can support you and our children. You're right, it's soon…but if what we just did results in a baby, I'll be the happiest man in the world."

Blythe studied him. "You're serious."

"Dead serious."

"You're a strange man," she blurted. "Most men would be freaking out and demanding I go and take the morning-after pill right about now."

"Fuck them. This is us. I love you. You love me. Why would I freak out about you carrying my child? Why do you think I bought this house? I want kids—lots of kids. I want them to be really close in age too so they can be best friends. I missed growing up with my sisters. I was already twelve when Emma was born."

"Sawyer," Blythe said weakly. The thought that the man bracing himself above her wanted kids, lots of them, was making her ovaries explode. Maybe not the best analogy at the moment, but he was seriously blowing her mind.

"Do you want kids?" he asked.

"Well, yeah."

"Then what's the problem?"

Blythe thought about it for a second, then shrugged. "People usually date for a while, then they get engaged. Then married. Then they have a rational discussion about children and if they're ready for them and how many they might want. *Then* they go about trying to have those children."

"So we're different. Who cares?" was Sawyer's response.

Blythe stared at him, then smiled. Then she was laughing. She felt his dick inside her twitch when she clenched around him as she laughed. But when he pulled back, then pressed back inside, her laughter died.

"Fuck, you're so wet," Sawyer said, more to himself than her.

"That's because you lubricated me so good," Blythe said dryly.

"You feel amazing," he went on. "So hot and tight." He rested his elbows on the carpet next to her head as his hips rhythmically pumped up and down.

"I thought we needed to get my stuff moved in," Blythe said breathlessly.

"After," Sawyer said.

"Okay. After."

Blythe blocked out everything but the feel of the man she loved inside her.

It was a couple hours later before they managed to get back to Sophie's to pick up the rest of her things. They'd made love on the floor of the future nursery once more, then Sawyer pulled her into his huge shower in the master bathroom and made love to her again. Then he'd made them lunch, and after they'd eaten, he'd laid her out on the dining room table and proceeded to make her come with his mouth and fingers two more times. And throwing caution to the wind, they'd not used any condoms while they'd made love.

That night, as she lay in Sawyer's bed, in his arms, in his house, Blythe reflected on her life. She'd been through some shit, but by some miracle, here she was. Sleeping with the man she loved, his come drying on her inner thighs, sore as all get out from all the lovemaking they'd done, but happier than she'd been in her entire life.

She knew as well as anyone that everything could come crashing down, but she'd also learned to take each day as it came. She'd live for the moment, and if things went to shit, at least she'd have the memories of how happy she was right this second to keep her going.

Look, Mom. Things worked out after all...just like you always told me they would.

CHAPTER FIFTEEN

*B*lythe knew Sawyer wasn't thrilled she'd insisted on coming with him when he went to check the shelters for Hope, but he'd finally agreed to let her accompany him to the one she'd used most often. She couldn't help but be secretly amused when he scowled at every man they passed. She had the insane thought that being homeless would've been much better with Sawyer by her side. She wouldn't have had to constantly be on alert. No one would've been able to sneak up behind her, and she would've been able to go to the front of the food line every night simply because the scowl on Sawyer's face would've scared everyone away.

She thought about Tadd and Louise. She'd often wondered how in the world the older couple had managed on the streets all the years they were homeless, but having Sawyer with her helped answer that question. Tadd wasn't exactly young, but he was still very protective of his wife, and that protectiveness projected itself clearly. No one messed with her, because messing with Louise meant messing with Tadd.

"You okay?" Sawyer asked as they walked into the large cafeteria of the shelter.

She looked up at him and smiled. "I'm good."

He'd been checking on her every couple of minutes. It was sweet, but it was also getting annoying. "I'll let you know if I'm not, all right?"

"Mmmm," he said, not really answering her.

Blythe figured it was the best she was going to get at the moment, so she decided to go with it. She glanced around the large room, looking for Hope and Billy. She didn't immediately see them, but that didn't mean a lot. It was still early. Even though the shelters filled up quickly, many times people wouldn't come until later. Once you were in for the night, you were in. And it could get claustrophobic.

She tried not to feel self-conscious as she walked to the office door in one of the corners of the large room. It wasn't that Blythe was wearing eight-hundred-dollar stilettos and designer clothes, but it was obvious she was an outsider now. First, her clothes were clean. Second, she wasn't carrying all her belongings with her. And third, Sawyer had decided to wear his Station 7 polo shirt and navy pants…his uniform of sorts.

Blythe knocked on the door and waited. Within a few moments, the door opened and a woman Blythe didn't recognize was standing there.

"Can I help you?"

"Hi. My name is Blythe Coopman, and I'm looking for a woman and her child. They're—"

The woman held up her hand, forestalling anything else Blythe was going to say. "I'm not allowed to give out any information about our patrons. If you have an official complaint, you'll have to—"

It was Blythe's turn to interrupt. "No, I don't have a complaint. I used to use this shelter, and she's my friend. I'm worried about her, and I'm in a position to help her and her child get off the streets."

The employee sighed and actually looked bored. It irritated Blythe, but she did her best to control her temper.

"As I said, we're not allowed to give out any information about the people we serve here."

Blythe opened her mouth to respond, but Sawyer got there before her. "Look, we appreciate your confidentiality, but we aren't asking for anything out of line. My girlfriend simply wants to help her friend. Surely you can understand that and support it, right?"

The woman didn't look swayed in the least by Sawyer's words.

"We're not allowed to give out—"

Sawyer wrapped his arm around Blythe's waist and pulled her away from the door even as the woman was still speaking. "Come on, baby. She's not going to help us. We'll just keep looking."

Blythe nodded and allowed herself to be led away from the completely unhelpful employee.

They walked around the room and Blythe tried to talk to a few of the men and women there, but they either ignored her or said they hadn't seen Hope and Billy.

Sighing in disappointment, Blythe stood with Sawyer on the sidewalk outside the shelter.

"What now?" Sawyer asked.

"There's another shelter a couple of blocks away," Blythe told him. "We could check there."

Sawyer started to lead her to the parking garage where he'd left his Jeep, but she stopped him with a hand on his arm. "We can walk. It's not far."

"Baby, I'm not sure I want you walking around down here. No one knows where those two assholes are who attacked you."

She appreciated his concern, but she knew this

area better than he ever would. If it was dark, he'd have a reason to be worried, but during the day the area was pretty safe. "It's fine," she told him. "It's broad daylight, and it's only a couple blocks. Besides," she said, smiling up at him, "you're with me. We'll be fine."

He blinked, then shook his head in exasperation. "I'm thrilled you trust me that much, but I'm not exactly the Hulk."

She smiled wider then tried to explain. "I know that just because you're with me doesn't mean something can't happen. But I feel safer when you're around."

Sawyer looked at her for a long moment, then pulled her into his arms. He kissed her hard and briefly before grabbing her hand. "Fine. But if I tell you to do something, like run, you do it without arguing. Got it?"

"Of course." As if. There was no way she was going to run away if someone jumped them.

He shook his head again, as if he knew what she was thinking, but didn't call her on it. He simply started off down the sidewalk in the direction she indicated, making sure she was on the inside, away from the street. It was a protective gesture, and pure Sawyer.

They didn't say much as they walked to the next

shelter. Blythe remembered taking this walk on countless occasions. When one shelter was full she'd always try another, but without much hope. And most of the time she was turned away at the next shelter too.

They passed an alley, and Blythe couldn't help but stop and stare down it.

"What?" Sawyer asked. "Did you see something?"

Blythe shook her head and said softly, "This was my favorite alley to sleep in. There are two big trash bins in the back. I could slide under them and be completely hidden from view. I'd lie there and watch people walking back and forth out here on the sidewalk, and they never knew I was there. Most of the time it was comforting, but sometimes that invisibility got to me."

Sawyer's arms wrapped around her from behind and he rested his chin on her shoulder. "I'm sorry that happened to you," he said quietly. "But you don't ever have to worry about that again. I'm here. Our friends are here. You aren't invisible, baby. Never again."

"What if we don't find Hope? Living out here was bad for me. I can't imagine what it's like for a woman with a child. I'm not a mother, but I know I would do whatever I could to keep my child safe, warm, and fed."

"We're going to find her. If not today, we'll try again. We won't stop looking for her," Sawyer vowed.

Blythe nodded. "Thank you."

"What are you thanking me for?" Sawyer asked.

She turned in his arms and burrowed into him. "For being you. For not being disgusted with who I was. For what I did. For being there for me. For loving me."

"You don't ever have to thank me for any of those things, Blythe. They just are. Just like the air we breathe and the water we drink."

She looked up at him and smiled. "I don't know what I did to deserve you, but I thank God every day for you."

"Just as I do you, baby," Sawyer returned. "Come on, let's get going. I can't say I particularly like hanging outside a dark alley with you, reminiscing about how awful your previous life was."

Blythe couldn't help it. She giggled. It was hard to believe she could actually laugh at anything that had to do with her life on the streets, but Sawyer gave her that ability. She shifted until she was at his side and kept her arm around his waist. "Lead on, Mr. Hulk."

"Jesus," he said, rolling his eyes. "I'm going to regret saying that, aren't I?"

Blythe didn't answer; just laid her head on his shoulder and grinned as they walked down the street.

* * *

Unbeknownst to the couple, a man was in the exact spot Blythe reminisced about so fondly. Lying under the trash bins in a drunken stupor, he eventually noticed them standing in the mouth of the alley.

He narrowed his eyes and tried to focus. He silently crawled out from under the trash bin and, keeping to the shadows, moved closer.

Yes, it was her.

Dog had spread the word that if anyone saw the bitch who'd dared interfere in his business and who hurt his friend, he was to be notified. He'd made it known that whoever spotted her, and got word to him, would be rewarded.

To the man skulking along the edge of the alley, that meant booze and drugs. And he needed both. Badly.

He followed the couple at a safe distance, gesturing to another homeless man who he sometimes got stoned with, dreaming about the high he was going to enjoy later with the reward he was sure to receive.

Within minutes, word was spreading from drunk to druggie to drunk that the woman Dog was searching for was on his turf.

The second Blythe and Squirrel walked into the next homeless shelter, a woman who was standing off to the side squealed and came running toward her.

Squirrel stepped in front of Blythe instinctively. He felt her hands on his waist, trying to push him aside, but he refused to budge.

"Sawyer, I know her. It's okay," Blythe said as she continued to try to move him.

At her words, Squirrel reluctantly stepped aside, but kept his hand on the small of her back as she greeted the other woman.

"Blythe! Oh my God, it's so good to see you!" the homeless woman said.

"You too, Gladys!"

They hugged, and when they pulled back, Gladys asked, "Where have you been? You've been gone *forever*—but you look good! I was so worried about you after I heard what Dog and Tweek had done. What happened?"

Squirrel tuned out Blythe's response as his gaze swept the room. He wasn't comfortable with Blythe being back here. He didn't like her remembering what she'd had to do while living on the streets. He didn't like seeing firsthand what she'd gone through.

And the back of his neck had been tingling ever since they'd left the first shelter.

It didn't help that, as he looked around, all he saw were people looking at them. Some glanced away when he caught them staring, but others didn't drop their hostile glares when he met their eyes. Squirrel wished he'd asked one of the guys to come with him. Maybe Moose. The man was huge, and no one would even think about harassing them if he was there.

"Have you seen Hope and Billy?" Blythe asked Gladys.

"Yeah, they were here yesterday."

Blythe put her hand on the other woman's arm. "Were they okay? How did they look? Is Billy dealing with what happened?"

Gladys gave her a sad smile. "I don't know. I mean, Hope smiled at me and said hello, but that's about it. She's been keeping to herself, not talking to anyone. She and her boy sit in one of the far corners and talk only to each other."

"Probably smart," Blythe muttered. "Can you give them a message for me? Tell them I've been looking for them? I really need to talk to them." She looked up at Squirrel for a second, then told Gladys, "I've got a place for them to live. My friend Sophie has a house. I've been staying there but I don't need it anymore. She said Hope and Billy could move in."

"That's great news!" Gladys exclaimed.

"Yeah. But I need to find them first," Blythe said.

"Of course."

Gladys looked over Blythe's shoulder then, and suddenly slunk away from the two of them just as they heard a man say, "Squirrel? That you?"

Blythe and Squirrel both turned at the same time upon hearing the low, masculine greeting.

Calder Stonewall stood there. He was wearing a huge white apron, which was stained with something brown, and was holding a serving spoon.

"Hey, man," Squirrel said, holding out his hand but not moving away from Blythe.

Calder came forward and the two men shook hands. Calder nodded his head at Blythe in greeting.

"What are you doing here?" she asked.

Calder chuckled and looked down at the apron he was wearing then back up at her. "Well, I'm tempted to say I was wandering around looking for things to stir and happened upon this place, but I don't think you'd believe me."

Blythe blushed and shook her head even as she chuckled.

"I'm volunteering," Calder said. "After meeting you and hearing your story, I realized that I really wanted to help more. I've been lucky, and others aren't so fortunate. Serving food isn't much but it's something I can do right now."

"It means a lot," Blythe said immediately.

Calder shrugged. "So that's why *I'm* here. Why are you two here?"

"I'm looking for my friend Hope and her son, Billy. Gladys said they were here yesterday. Sophie said they could move into her old house."

"Have you seen her?" Blythe asked Calder. "She's about my height, with long dark red hair. Green eyes. Her son is seven and has red hair too. I mean, has she been here today while you've been serving?"

"Not today. But, Blythe...apparently Gladys has been off her meds for quite a while," he said.

"I know, but she seems really good today," Blythe said.

Calder's voice lowered. "I overheard the staff saying yesterday that she was getting worse, not better. She's becoming more and more forgetful. She thinks her daughter is going to come and get her this afternoon."

"Oh," Blythe said sadly. "So she probably hasn't seen Hope and Billy?"

Calder shrugged. "I'm guessing...no."

"Well, shit."

"You overheard the staff yesterday? How much time are you spending down here?" Squirrel asked his friend.

Calder smiled a crooked smile. "I had a few days off. Was bored. Thought I'd come down and help. What can you tell me about Hope? I can keep my eye out for her."

"She's had it rough. An ex beat the crap out of her and she ended up on the streets. Billy was abducted by that child-abuser guy who kidnapped Milena, and I'm just worried about him. I need to find them so they can be safe."

"If I see them, I'll talk to her. Pass on a message from you that you're looking for her."

"Go easy," Squirrel told his friend, "but don't let them leave. Call Blythe and let her talk to Hope if you have to. So she knows you aren't out to do her harm."

Calder nodded. "I will." Then he turned to Blythe. "I'll find them."

"She's not going to trust you," she said.

"I know."

"It's going to be hard to convince her to go anywhere with you. Especially because of Billy."

"Yep. I know."

"Maybe tell her you're a medical examiner. No,

tell her you're a cop and you want to help her. Shit, no—that won't work. Her ex is a cop. She doesn't trust them."

Calder put his hand on Blythe's arm. "I got this. I'll deliver your friend and her son to you safe and sound. Okay?"

"Okay. Thanks. I appreciate it."

"No thanks necessary. I can't stand it when assholes abuse their power. It's bad enough that she was beaten by her husband, a man who should've had her back no matter what, but when he's also a cop? That just pisses me off."

Squirrel remained quiet and examined his friend. As one of the MEs for the county, he was frequently called out to scenes with victims that had passed away. But Squirrel had never seen this side of him. His free hand was clenched in a fist and he was frowning. Calder was older than all the firefighters he hung out with, but it was obvious looking at him now, being in his forties didn't mean he wasn't willing or able to protect those who he thought needed it.

Calder turned to Squirrel. "I haven't been volunteering here long, but word is that those two thugs are still looking for Blythe. Keep your eye out."

"Will do. I think we're done here. Blythe?" Squirrel asked.

"I really wanted to wait around a bit and see if Hope came in. I know that Calder will be on the lookout, but it'll be hard for him to earn her trust. I know her, Sawyer. Please?"

Squirrel sighed. The tingly sensation on the back of his neck hadn't abated, in fact, it had gotten stronger, but it was probably because of everyone staring at them. There hadn't been one confirmed sighting of Hope or her son, but he didn't have the heart to say no to Blythe. "One hour, baby. Then we really do need to go."

"Perfect. Thanks, Sawyer."

He leaned down and kissed her cheek before whispering, "You don't have to thank me, baby. I'd do anything to make you happy."

She beamed up at him.

"At that, I'll just go back to what I was doing," Calder said. "Let me know before you go. I'll walk with you back to your car. I don't like the look of the crowd in here today."

Squirrel looked Calder in the eyes for a long moment before nodding. He'd be an idiot to refuse help with the way he was feeling. If it was just him, he would deal with it, but since Blythe was with him, he accepted as graciously as he could. "Thanks. One hour. Come on, baby," Squirrel said, taking her hand in his. "Let's sit. It's getting creepy, having everyone stare at us."

"Now you know how I felt every day when I was here," Blythe muttered.

Squirrel's jaw tensed at that, but he didn't say anything. He'd sympathized with her, but he couldn't *empathize*. He hadn't been in her shoes. But even the short amount of time he'd spent in the shelter made him realize exactly how stressful it had to have been for her. Everyone was on edge, the air filled with desperation. He could imagine that if he was carrying a bag and put it down, that it'd be gone the second he turned his back.

It was a miracle Blythe had managed to hold on to his cell phone for as long as she had. That was the kind of thing that could be pawned for quite a bit of money. Money someone could use to buy drugs, alcohol, or food. Three things that were probably in high demand on the streets.

Squirrel stayed by Blythe's side as they walked over to the corner. He made sure to sit between her and the rest of the room. Everything inside him was telling him to get out now, but he stayed put. The last thing he wanted to do was freak Blythe out. It was bad enough she was reliving one of the worst times in her life. She didn't need him being paranoid on top of it.

Besides, he wanted to see if the mysterious Hope would turn up as much as Blythe did. He didn't like the little he'd heard about her situation, and the sooner she and her son were safe inside Sophie's house, the better. He realized that he couldn't save everyone, but since Hope was someone Blythe liked, he wanted to get her and her son to safety as soon as possible.

Looking at his watch, Squirrel reassured himself that it was only an hour. Sixty minutes, then they would be out of there. He was proud of Blythe for wanting to get her degree and help others who had been in her situation, but he wasn't thrilled about her working day in and day out in a place like this.

Taking a deep breath, Squirrel tried not to fidget. He eyed his watch once more. Fifty-nine minutes to go.

Word could travel fast on the streets when needed. Within fifteen minutes, Dog had been notified that the bitch he was looking for was in the shelter. Within twenty-five minutes, Dog had gotten ahold of Tweek and two other men who were excited about the prospect of joining in the gangbang Dog had planned.

Within forty minutes, the men had placed themselves strategically outside the shelter in all directions, so no matter which way the cunt went, she'd end up in their clutches.

As far as Dog was concerned, payback was a bitch, and there was one cunt who was going to find out the hard way never to get between Dog and something he wanted.

He crouched in an alley behind a piece of plywood and rubbed his hand over his crotch. His dick was hard as he fantasized about what was about to happen. He'd get first crack at the bitch, and he didn't care what the others did with her once he was done…as long as she didn't live to interfere with his business ever again.

CHAPTER SIXTEEN

"I guess she's not going to show up," Blythe said. Her shoulders slumped with disappointment.

"We'll find her," Sawyer said with conviction. "She has to be somewhere. I'm sure Calder will talk to the people who work and volunteer here and tell them to be on the lookout too. He'll contact us as soon as someone sees her, then we can come down and get her."

Blythe looked up at Sawyer. "But what if it's too late? What if she's lying dead somewhere and Billy is scared to leave her side? What if I'm the only one who can convince her and she disappears for good after Calder talks to her? What if she's—"

"Baby, stop," Sawyer ordered, taking her by the shoulders and gently shaking her. "Don't borrow trouble. You said yourself that you didn't always make it to the shelters. She sounds as if she's pretty street savvy. And even if Calder can't convince her, he won't let her leave before you get here."

Blythe took a deep breath. "You're right. I'm sorry. I'm just so worried about her."

"I know. Come on. Let's go home and see what Beth ordered for you today."

"When is she going to get tired of buying me stuff? Can't you tell her to stop?"

Sawyer chuckled. "Uh…never, and it wouldn't do any good. She does what she wants, and what she wants is for you to have the things you need. And even the stuff you don't."

"But it's too much," Blythe said. "I don't need that leather jacket she ordered for me. It's Texas, for goodness sake. And I definitely don't need all those DVDs she's sent. I know I missed a lot of good TV shows, but it's over the top."

"She likes you," Sawyer told her gently. "She feels helpless to assist you in other ways, so it's her way of showing you that you're a part of their circle of friends."

Blythe thought about that. It was true that she'd received a ton of texts from the other women. Adeline, Penelope, Sophie, Beth, and even Quinn had been texting her nonstop. It was sometimes too much, but mostly it was…nice. Not only that, but Sawyer's sisters were still contacting her constantly, and even his mom had sent a text or two.

It was crazy how many people she talked to on a daily basis now. When she was homeless, it had been mostly just Sawyer.

Deciding to let it go, Blythe looked up at him. "Have I told you how much I appreciate you?"

He grinned. "Yes."

She shook her head. "I seriously don't know where I'd be if—"

Sawyer put his finger over her lips. "Hush. None of that. Things work out the way they're supposed to work out. Come on, let's get out of here. I want to feed you, something better than the fare they're serving here. Then I want to take you home and spoil you."

"You always spoil me. I don't need anything, Sawyer," Blythe insisted.

"I know. That's part of the reason it's so fun to do things for you."

She smiled up at him and shook her head in exasperation. "What am I going to do with you?"

"Love me." It wasn't a question.

"Yeah, that's a given."

He leaned forward and kissed her forehead, keeping his lips on her skin for a long moment before pulling away. "Come on, baby. This place makes me nervous."

They stood and Sawyer helped her up with a hand at her elbow. She saw him look over at the serving line. Calder wasn't anywhere to be seen, but one of the employees saw where he was looking and gestured to a set of swinging doors, holding up a finger.

"Dang it, I just want to go," Sawyer said impatiently.

Blythe turned to him and put a hand on his chest. Wanting to take his mind off of the shelter, she stood on tiptoes and put her mouth next to his ear. "Know what I want?" She didn't wait for him to answer. "You haven't given me a chance to taste you. I want you on your back in bed, and I want to explore...and play. I want to take you in my—"

"Sorry about that, guys," Calder said from next to them.

Blythe jerked in surprise, but Sawyer put his hand on the small of her back, holding her steady against him. His voice was husky as he answered his friend.

"It's okay. We're ready."

Blythe wanted to laugh because she could feel how ready Sawyer was. His erection was hard against her lower stomach. She'd said the words to distract him, but now that she'd begun to think about it, the thought of lowering to her knees and sucking him off wouldn't leave her mind.

Sawyer gestured for Calder to proceed them and Blythe couldn't keep the small chuckle inside. She shivered as Sawyer leaned down and whispered in her ear, "You're gonna pay for that, baby."

She looked up at him coyly. "I hope so."

He grinned and turned her toward the door. "Come on, let's get out of here."

Blythe followed Calder and felt Sawyer at her back. They walked out of the shelter and turned right to walk the few blocks to the garage where he'd left his vehicle.

"I'll drop you off at your car," Sawyer told Calder.

"Sounds good," was his response.

It was refreshing to be around people who did things for each other and didn't expect anything in return.

They walked a block and a half and talked about nothing in particular. Calder asked for a few more details about Hope. He said he wanted to make sure he didn't miss her when she did eventually show up. He also seemed very interested in Billy. If he was attending school, how Blythe thought he was doing after being abducted, that sort of thing.

Blythe was feeling good about how the day had

gone, even if she hadn't found Hope. She knew in her gut that between Calder, Sawyer, and the rest of the guys, they wouldn't stop until they'd found her, and got her and her son to safety.

She'd just turned to look up at Sawyer and ask him something—when all hell broke loose.

One second, they were all walking down the sidewalk, and the next, Blythe found herself in a chokehold. She couldn't see who was behind her, but she could smell him. Sour beer and body odor. The combination made her cough and her eyes water.

Both her hands went up to the arm at her neck and she tried to pull at it so she could get some air, but whoever had her wasn't loosening his hold.

Her eyes swung up and caught Sawyer's.

He. Was. Pissed.

He wasn't looking at her, but rather at whoever held her. Not only was the man cutting off her air, she could feel the point of a knife against the skin at her side. She was dragged backward into one of the many alleys in the city. With every step she took, Sawyer's jaw got harder and harder.

It was weird how no one said a word—but they didn't have to. There was no doubt in her mind that Dog and Tweek had found her.

Squirrel had looked away from Blythe for two seconds to respond to something Calder had said, and in those two seconds, someone had come up behind them and grabbed Blythe around the neck and was threatening her with a knife. He would've lashed out at him if it wasn't for the blade—and was still seriously considering it, when suddenly they were surrounded by three more men.

They weren't big, but they were desperate. If Moose was with him, Squirrel figured they probably could've taken on all of the men. But he wasn't. He recognized Dog from the description Blythe had given the officer when she was in the hospital after she'd been attacked. And Dog had Blythe in a head-lock so tight, he could see her face turning red.

Squirrel could almost taste the hatred in the air. He felt Calder come up behind him and they squared off with the thugs who had jumped them. But he knew these weren't regular thugs. Whatever feeling he'd had in the shelter had obviously been spot on.

Squirrel refused to look at Blythe again. He knew if he did, he'd lose it. So he kept his eyes on the man who was holding her. He had his arm around her neck, and the knife in his other hand was way too close to Blythe for comfort. At the moment, it was aimed at her side, but he could easily shift and cut her throat if he wanted to.

No one said a word as they moved deeper into an alley. He felt as if he had tunnel vision. Squirrel knew he should be worried about the other three men flanking them, but his only concern was Blythe and the asshole who held her.

When they were halfway down the alley, Squirrel broke the silence. "Dog, I presume?"

The man holding Blythe smirked. "So you've heard of me."

There was so much Squirrel wanted to say, but he didn't want to antagonize the jerk. Not while Blythe was at his mercy. "What do you want?" he asked in a low, deadly voice.

"Me and this bitch have unfinished business," Dog growled.

Squirrel's mind was whirring with possible next steps. He could bum rush Dog, but he might sink the knife into Blythe's side before he got close. Squirrel could turn and fight the men surrounding him and Calder, but that would also leave Blythe vulnerable. Dog could slink off with her while he was otherwise occupied.

"Let her go," he demanded, more to kill time than anything else.

As expected, Dog refused. "No."

"Look," Squirrel said. "Nothing good will come of you hurting Blythe. She's got friends, lots of them. In high places. The FBI, Texas Rangers, SAPD. If something happens to her, you'll never be able to go back to your normal life again. They'll never stop hunting you and your friends. You'll end up in prison—and I can guarantee it won't be a walk in the park. You're a small fish, Dog. Let her go, and I can try to make sure that doesn't happen."

"Whatever, asshole," Dog scoffed. "This bitch interfered in my business. She has to pay."

Calder spoke up then. "You ever been in jail?"

Squirrel wasn't sure who Calder was talking to but he didn't take his gaze from Dog.

"It's nothing like being out here on the streets," his friend went on. "Out here, you have friends who have your back, but in there, you're on your own. And I've got people who will guarantee that."

"Fuck. Tweek, man, let's go," one of the thugs surrounding them said.

"Don't listen to him," Tweek told Dog, ignoring the other man. "The bitch cut me up! He's just trying to scare you."

"I'm not lying," Calder insisted. "I had an inmate on my table the other day. I'm a medical examiner for the county. I get all the dead bodies and have to autopsy them. Guy had forty-three stab wounds. And you want to know what he was stabbed with?" Calder didn't wait for a response. "A fork. He was jumped by five other inmates and forked to death. The wounds weren't deep; he actually lived for a week after the attack. He died of infection. Apparently, the other inmates had covered the forks with their shit before stabbing him. You want that to be you?"

Squirrel had no idea if Calder was making that story up or not, but one of the three men who'd surrounded them obviously believed it, because his footsteps as he ran away echoed in the alley around them.

"Roach!" Tweek yelled after the man. "Fuck!"

"Let her go," Squirrel ordered Dog again.

"Fuck you. Me and her have a date. I'm gonna fuck her in every hole. Then my friends are gonna take their turns. She's gonna learn her lesson about not butting in where she doesn't belong. And everyone else is gonna learn that same lesson. *No one* fucks with Dog. These are *my* streets. I own them."

Squirrel's eyes dropped to Blythe's for the first time. She looked terrified...but there was a hint of anger there too.

Good. If she was too scared to do anything to help herself, it would make this harder.

He took a step forward, and Dog took a step back.

Squirrel opened his mouth to respond when he heard a commotion behind him.

"Fuck!" he heard Tweek shout before another unknown voice thundered out.

"These aren't *your* streets, motherfucker. And we're getting mighty tired of you thinking they are."

Squirrel took his eyes off of Dog for the first time and turned to the side, just enough to look at the newcomers.

Standing in a semi-circle around them were six rough-looking men. They were all wearing blue and each had a gun in his hand. The men's heads were shaved, and all of them were muscular. They were all white, and obviously members of a gang.

Calder immediately took a few steps to the side and put his back against the wall of the alley, holding his hands out to his sides, showing he was unarmed.

His actions were telling. *These* were men to be concerned about. Not Dog and his gang of wannabe hangers-on. Squirrel knew without a doubt they could take him and Calder down with no problem. He just hoped it didn't come to that.

Squirrel wanted to follow Calder's example, get out of the way and let them do what they wanted with Dog and his friends, but he couldn't, not with Blythe still in danger.

"This doesn't concern you, Blue," Dog said with a

little less swagger in his tone. "This bitch done me wrong."

"What'd she do?" the man named Blue asked.

"She interfered with my business."

"And what was that?"

"I had a target culled from the herd and was making my move when she butted in, and they were able to get away."

"Hmmm," Blue murmured, stroking his temple with the muzzle of his pistol. "So you were trying to rob someone in *my* territory when you know how I feel about that. I've told you time and time again to cut that shit out. And further, how'd she butt in? She's a skinny little bitch. Can't imagine her being able to get the drop on you."

"She didn't," Dog countered, obviously pissed at the innuendo, that he wasn't man enough to handle her. "She surprised me and Tweek, cut up his neck, and my targets ran while we were dealing with her."

"That's my woman," Squirrel said, venturing into the conversation. "She was homeless a while back and sleeping under a trash bin when she saw Dog and his friends robbing a tourist couple. She decided to get involved. Got a few knife wounds as thanks."

Blue looked over at Squirrel. He eyed him up and down, staring for a long moment at the Station 7 logo on his shirt before speaking. "Homeless?"

Squirrel couldn't read anything in the gang member's tone but took a risk anyway. "Yeah. Her mom died. Cancer. She couldn't pay the medical bills and got kicked out of her apartment. She'd already lost her job because she had to stay home and take care of her dying mother. Ended up on the streets."

"And you *let* her?" Blue asked.

"I didn't know her then," Squirrel said calmly. "But I know her now. She's mine."

"Why are you down here if she's yours? Not exactly the place to be taking an afternoon stroll. Especially with people like him around."

Squirrel wanted to roll his eyes at the guy's statement. As if Dog was the dangerous one here. Blue and his gang seemed to be ten times the threat Dog and Tweek were. But he'd asked a valid question. "She's got a friend she's concerned about. Also homeless. With a kid. She wanted to find and help them."

"She interfered!" Dog shouted. "And she cut Tweek's neck! Stupid bitch doesn't know her place."

Blue turned back to Dog. "Give her to me," he ordered in a low, deadly tone.

Squirrel tensed but kept quiet. It was one thing to have to fight Dog and Tweek for Blythe, but fighting the six gang members would be almost impossible.

"Fuck you!" Dog spat. "She's *mine*. I found her

first." He was acting as if he really were a dog fighting over a meaty bone.

"Let her go right now—or face the consequences," Blue repeated.

Squirrel heard another scuffle and saw that Tweek and the other guy—he still didn't know his name—had tried to run. But they'd easily been caught by two of Blue's gang members. They had guns pointed at both of their heads.

This was seriously getting out of hand, and Squirrel had no idea what his next step should be. He glanced at Calder, but his friend's eyes were glued to Blue.

"We've been meaning to deal with you for a while now," Blue said. "Let the bitch go."

Dog brought the knife up to Blythe's throat, replacing his arm with the blade. "Back off, Blue! I'll slit her throat."

Squirrel took a step toward Dog then, his eyes focused on the sharp edge of the blade at Blythe's throat. A thin line of blood welled up as Dog took a step backward, forcing Blythe to do the same.

Blue also took a step forward. Squirrel could see him out of the corner of his eye.

The air was thick with tension and anticipation as everyone waited to see which man would make the next move. Dog, to kill Blythe; Blue, to shoot

Dog; or Squirrel, to bum-rush Dog, hoping to get to him before he had the chance to run the knife across Blythe's throat.

Interestingly enough, it was *Blythe* who made the first move.

Her hands had come up to cling to Dog's arm when he'd put the knife at her throat...

Now, with a grunt, she shoved his forearm and threw herself to the side at the same time.

Squirrel started moving before she began to fall, as he'd been watching her closely. He was going to make sure Dog couldn't get to her after she was on the ground but Blue acted before Dog could take a step.

The sound of the pistol going off was loud in the alley, echoing off the walls and making Squirrel's ears ring.

With no regard for his own safety, Squirrel didn't even slow his movements. He threw himself over Blythe and rolled, holding her tightly in his arms. They ended up next to one of the brick walls and he caged her body with his, trying to keep every inch of her covered.

No one said a word for a second—then all hell broke loose. Tweek started yelling and the other men in the gang yelled right back. Then Squirrel heard Blue's low, pissed-off voice over all the others.

"This is our turf, got it? You don't rob tourists, because they're *ours*. You don't sell drugs, because that's *our* job. You don't do *anything* without our permission. You don't like it? You can fucking go somewhere else. Yeah?"

"Yeah, yeah, I got it!" Tweek acquiesced quickly.

"Get the fuck out of here," Blue ordered.

Squirrel heard footsteps running away, but he didn't take his eyes from Blythe. She was curled into his chest, ducked down so all he could see was the top of her head. He scooted back a fraction and rolled her to her back. He eyed her throat, making sure she didn't need immediate medical attention. Thoughts of her jugular being sliced open were at the forefront of his mind. She had a small cut, but it wasn't gushing blood. Sighing in relief, he met her eyes for the first time. "Are you okay?"

"I…I think so. You?"

"I'm good. Fuck, Blythe…*fuck*."

She began to shake then and buried her head in his chest once more, holding on to him as if she'd never let go.

"She good?" Blue asked from above them.

Squirrel didn't care that he was lying in who knew what. Wetness was seeping through his pants, but it didn't matter. Not when he had Blythe safe in his arms.

But the danger wasn't over. The man standing over them wasn't exactly a saint. Yeah, he'd saved Blythe, but he was still extremely dangerous.

Squirrel turned his head, refusing to loosen his hold on Blythe. "She's good. Thank you."

Blue stared at him for a long moment, his expression unreadable. "That sucks about her mom. My ma was a good woman. She didn't deserve the shit she went through either."

Squirrel nodded but didn't speak.

"When I was twelve, our house burned down. Molotov cocktail thrown through the window by a rival gang. Firefighters came and found me and Ma hiding in her room. They got us out. We would've died if they hadn't done what they did. Consider this my payback."

Squirrel understood. They'd been extremely lucky Blue felt he owed a marker to the nameless firefighters from so long ago who had saved him.

Sirens sounded in the distance and Blue motioned to his buddies with his head. Without another word, Blue jammed his gun in the pocket of his jeans and nodded at Squirrel. "Glad you're all right," he said to Blythe, who was now peeking up at him from her position in Squirrel's arms. "A bit of advice...get out of here and don't look back. The streets aren't any place for a good woman like yourself."

Blythe didn't move, didn't speak. Squirrel didn't think she even blinked.

Blue went on, "If I run across your friend and her son, I'll give her the same advice. I'll tell her to go to the shelter over on Fifth and Main and call her friend…" His voice trailed off and his eyebrows went up in question.

Blythe looked up at the dangerous gang member and said, "Blythe. Tell her to call Blythe."

Blue nodded, then spun on his heel and walked back down the alley the way he'd come. The rest of his entourage following along behind him.

Calder came over to them then and put his hand on Squirrel's back. "You okay?"

"Yeah."

"Come on, let me help you up."

Squirrel reluctantly disengaged from Blythe and stood, then he quickly helped her to her feet and took her back into his arms. "We're going to have to explain that," he told Calder, nodding toward Dog's dead body lying in the alley behind them.

"Yeah. But the fact that Blythe had a run-in with him before, and we were witnesses this time, will work in our favor. I have a feeling Blue knows how to handle himself when questioned by the police."

Squirrel nodded.

"I'm going to call Quint and Hayden. They might be able to smooth things over quickly as well," Calder said.

Squirrel nodded again. "And tell them to get an ambulance here for Blythe, would ya?"

"On it."

Blythe shook her head. "I'm okay, Sawyer. I don't need an ambulance."

"Tough," he told her. "You're getting one."

She sighed but asked Calder, "Were you lying about the forks?"

He grimaced. "Unfortunately, no."

"Gross," she whispered.

"Yeah. It definitely was," Calder agreed before stepping away to make his calls.

Squirrel put his hands on either side of her head and turned her face up to his. "Are you sure you're okay? He had a pretty good hold on you."

"I'm positive."

"I can't believe you did that. You could've gotten hurt, baby. He could've sliced your throat as you pulled away from him. You scared the shit out of me."

"He wasn't going to let me go," Blythe said with conviction. "That Blue guy was going to shoot him one way or another. I saw it in his eyes. I knew if I didn't get myself out of the way, I might be caught in the middle of whatever turf war they were having. I decided a cut in the process of getting away was better than being shot or having my jugular sliced open."

Squirrel couldn't disagree with her.

"I'm sorry I couldn't save you myself."

Blythe smiled then. "But you did."

"No, I didn't."

"Sawyer, you did," she insisted. "Without you here, the gang guy would've shot Dog without caring that I was in his way. He saw that you were a firefighter, and because of what happened to him and his mom, because *you* were here, he waited until he had a clear shot. So you did save me."

Squirrel didn't really believe her, but he wasn't going to argue. He wished he could've prevented her from being in Dog's clutches in the first place.

They stood there in that alley, a place where, in a different time, Blythe might've slept, to wait for the cops to arrive. And soaked in the relief of knowing they were both alive and relatively unscathed.

*T*wo weeks later, Blythe got home before Sawyer. They'd gotten back into a routine of sorts. Sawyer would drop her off at the library when he wasn't on shift, and when he was, Sophie would stop by and pick her up on her way to work. After Blythe worked her five-hour shift, Beth would pick her up and drop her off back at Sawyer's house…that is, if she didn't take her shopping or kidnap her for a meeting with the "girls."

Blythe mock-complained about those meetings with Penelope, Sophie, Adeline and, more often than not, Quinn, but the truth was that she loved them. She'd never had such close friends as them. The first time Blythe had been paid, she'd done what she'd promised herself she would—she'd bought everyone a round of drinks. Of course, then Sophie decided *she* wanted to buy a round. And Beth couldn't be left out. By the time their men had come to pick them up, they'd all been completely trashed at three in the afternoon.

Hope and Billy still hadn't been found, and Blythe was getting worried and scared about how they were doing and where they were. Calder had been going to the area where Blythe said they used to hang out, but so far he hadn't had any luck in finding them.

The cops had done an investigation into Dog's death and, with the help of security cameras at the entrance to the alley, Blue was now wanted for (another) murder, but Blythe figured he probably didn't care. It gave him more street cred.

Things between her and Sawyer were wonderful. They'd both been getting used to living with another person and, for the most part, had settled into their lives as a couple flawlessly. Sawyer was a bit too overprotective at times and had been way too willing to open his wallet anytime she casually mentioned liking something, but she'd done her best to rein him in.

Blythe loved the way Sawyer texted her when he was leaving the station on his way home. Loved how his eyes lit up the second he saw her when he walked in the door. Loved how he wrapped her in his arms and gave her the longest hug, as if they'd been separated for years rather than hours or days while he was on shift.

But she enjoyed simply lying in his arms most of all. After they made love, he'd turn her to him and she'd rest her ear on his chest and listen to the beating of his heart. She'd been without human contact for so long that feeling his arms around her meant that much more.

Their love life was as amazing as it had been their first time. Sawyer was a very attentive lover, making sure she was satisfied several times over before he saw to his own needs. He was sweet and loving, but Blythe was trying to make him understand that his pleasure was just as important to her as hers was to him.

She'd managed to convince him to let her have her way with him one night. She'd gotten him on his back and kissed every inch of his chest, played with his nipples just like he did with hers, and had been giving him what she'd thought was the most amazing blow job in the history of blow jobs...when without warning, he'd sat up, threw her on her back, entered her, and began to fuck her to within an inch of her life.

It had been *awesome*.

Of course, he'd been mortified that she hadn't

come before him and had spent the next two hours making up for that oversight. She'd tried to tell him that she'd gotten as much pleasure from making him lose control as anything else they'd done, but he wouldn't listen.

Blythe smiled as she remembered that night. Far be it from her to complain about a man who made her come multiple times.

There were times when they were both too tired to make love, but she didn't like those nights any less. He always held her close, and the intimacy of sleeping in his arms was almost as good as their sex life.

But tonight, Blythe had a special present for her man. Tomorrow, they were going over to his parents' house, and she wanted to give them her news at that time. But first Sawyer needed to know.

She fiddled around in the kitchen for a while, then wandered from room to room in his house impatiently. Finally, her phone vibrated with a text.

Squirrel: Heading out. Be home soon.

Blythe smiled and the butterflies started up in her stomach. She was nervous, but excited.

.   .   .

BC: *Drive safe. Love you.*

Blythe looked down at the phone in her hand. It was the same one Sawyer had accidentally given to her at that fire so many months ago. She knew eventually she'd have to get a new phone, but she loved this one. It had been her lifeline when she'd been on the streets and had brought Sawyer into her life. How could she not love it?

Ten minutes or so later, she heard a key in the lock at the front door. She waited in the kitchen and within seconds, Sawyer was there. He took her into his arms and gave her a bear hug.

"Hey, baby."

"Hey."

"How was your day?"

"Good. How was the rest of your shift?"

"Pretty boring, thankfully."

Blythe knew a boring shift was a good thing. It meant that no one was hurt or killed and that there hadn't been any fires.

"Are you all right?" Sawyer asked her.

Blythe grinned. She couldn't ever hide anything from her man.

"Yeah. I'm great. I have a surprise for you though."

His eyebrows rose in question.

Blythe decided not to drag it out. She was too excited and couldn't wait to see his reaction. "You know how I haven't been feeling that great lately? I went to the pharmacy and got a test today."

"Are you all right? What's wrong?"

"Nothing's wrong," she reassured him, taking hold of his hand and bringing it down to rest on her belly. "In fact, I'm not one hundred percent sure, but I think everything's right."

It took him a moment, but then his eyes widened so comically, Blythe couldn't help but giggle.

"Are you…oh my God, baby. You're pregnant?"

Blythe nodded. "We haven't been using any condoms and I guess I'm really fertile. Either that, or your sperm are Olympic swimmers."

"Holy shit," Sawyer said. Then he ordered, "Wait here," and rushed away.

Blythe blinked in surprise. That wasn't the response she thought she'd get when she told him he was going to be a father.

Within moments, Sawyer was back. He took hold of her hand and led her out of the kitchen and into the living area. He turned—and immediately got down on one knee.

He held her hand in his and looked up at her as he spoke.

"I love you, Blythe Coopman. When I realized that I'd accidentally left my phone in the pocket of that sweatshirt, I was pissed. I mean, it was my phone. But then I thought about how useful it could be to you. You should've seen me that first time you texted me back. I was ecstatic. I had worked so hard to get you to use it that, when you finally texted me, it seemed like I'd just accomplished something amazing.

"And it was. From that day on, you burrowed further and further into my heart. I love you, baby. You see *me*, the real me."

He reached into his pocket and pulled out a small box. He flipped it open, and Blythe gasped at the ring nestled in the velvet. It wasn't huge, but it wasn't small either. She looked at Sawyer with tears in her eyes. She couldn't believe this was happening.

"Will you marry me? Give me the chance to spoil you for the rest of our lives? I can't promise to never make a mistake or be a jerk, but I'll work extra hard to make sure you know that you're the most important person in my life. Always. I'll try to—"

"Yes!" Blythe said, interrupting him. "Yes, Sawyer. I'll marry you."

He smiled up at her. He picked up the ring and

dropped the box, not even looking where it landed. He kissed the finger on her left hand before sliding the ring onto it. He gazed at the diamond for a long moment before saying, "My sisters helped me find a ring we thought you'd like. I wanted to get a huge one that would make it clear you were taken, but they talked me out of it." Sawyer looked up at her then. "I know you want to work with the homeless, and buying a huge-ass ring probably wouldn't be the smartest thing I could do for you."

She loved that he had such confidence in her. It would be a long time before she could earn her degree, and even then, there was no guarantee she'd get a job where she wanted.

Blythe got down on her knees and pushed him back so he was sitting on his butt. She straddled his legs and clung to him. His arms went around her and they sat on the floor in their home for a long moment. Finally, Blythe pulled back and smiled.

"I love you, Sawyer. You were there for me when I had no one else. You kept me sane when I was on the streets. You were the reason I didn't give up. You're going to be an amazing dad because you're already an amazing brother, son, and friend. I can't wait to meet our child."

"Pregnant," he said in awe. "I can't believe it."

She raised her eyebrows at him. "Really? I mean,

it's not like we've done much to prevent this from happening."

"True." He grinned. "My plan has obviously worked. Give my phone to the beautiful woman, get her to trust me, rescue her from the streets, make her fall in love with me, get her pregnant, and then convince her to marry me."

Blythe smiled. "How many do you want?" she asked quietly.

"Three or four," Sawyer said without even pausing to think about it.

"Really?"

"Yeah. And as close together as possible. I loved having sisters but was sad that we weren't closer in ages. I want a brother who can be there to protect his sisters. I want girls who can pester their brothers. I want sisters who will drive each other crazy, but later in life will be each other's best friends."

Blythe swallowed hard, trying to control her emotions. "Okay."

"Okay?"

"Yeah, Sawyer. I'm okay with that. I want a big family. With you."

"God, I love you," Sawyer said, hugging her to him, then falling backward, holding her on top of him.

"I think we conceived that first day. Remember?

When you tackled me in that room upstairs? The baby's room? Maybe the spirit of that miscarried child was there, and helped."

"I like that thought," Sawyer told her. Then one hand pressed her against his growing erection and the other wandered up and under her shirt, brushing against her spine as he went. "I think we should celebrate."

"Yeah? How so? I know—we could call your parents," Blythe teased.

He shook his head. "I think tomorrow is soon enough for them to know. I have other plans for my fiancée."

She smiled even as she lowered her head. They kissed, and she could feel *his* smile against her lips. Blythe ground herself down on his cock as she pulled away. "We have a perfectly good bed upstairs…we should use it."

"No," Sawyer said immediately. "As soon as our first kid is born, it'll be harder and harder to make love whenever and wherever we want."

"True," Blythe said, even as she arched her back. Sawyer's hands had both snaked under her shirt and had undone her bra. "Here's good."

"I love you," Sawyer said reverently as he helped her take off her shirt.

"And I love you," Blythe responded.

Neither spoke anymore as they made love and celebrated their blessings right there on the floor of the living room.

Hours later, when Blythe was held tight in her future husband's arms, sated and content, she couldn't help but think she was the luckiest woman in the world, and that she wouldn't change one second of her life if it meant she'd end up right where she was. Pregnant, engaged, and wonderfully happy.

Calder jerked as the pager next to him began to vibrate. He sprang out of bed and reached for his jeans. He was used to being woken up at odd hours of the day and night. Dead bodies didn't have regular hours, and it was his job as medical examiner to study those bodies to figure out their cause of death. It wasn't glamorous, but it was interesting.

He worked with detectives across all agencies to investigate and help figure out how and when a person died.

Calder shoved his feet into his shoes and made a quick stop in the bathroom before heading out of his house. He checked his messages to see where he needed to go and saw an address downtown.

He'd been spending a lot of his time downtown recently. After hearing about Blythe's friend's plight, he'd wanted to help find her. Something about Hope and Billy's story tugged at his heartstrings. He wasn't normally one to be overly sentimental or sympathetic. Examining dead bodies for a living did that to him, he knew, but hearing that Hope was on the run from an abusive ex, who was also in law enforcement, pissed him off.

Protecting others was what he and his friends did. Abusing their power wasn't something any of them would ever consider, and the thought of someone else hiding behind a badge irked him.

But he'd been searching for weeks now, with no luck. He'd begun to think Hope and her son had left the area for good. And he couldn't blame them. Calder just hoped they'd found a safe place to go.

He drove to the area where the dead body had been found and, as he neared, saw the lights from the cop cars. He pulled up as close as he could, flashing his badge to the officers. He parked and picked up his medical bag and was escorted behind the yellow crime scene tape.

It was dark, and the few streetlights in the area didn't do much to penetrate the murky shadows of the night. His eyes immediately went to the body on the ground, which hadn't been covered. He was glad;

it was important to leave the scene completely untouched.

The crime scene techs would come and collect evidence soon, but all Calder was concerned about was the body. He could tell a lot about what happened simply by "listening" to what the deceased told him.

He took a step toward the body, his mind already whirring with possibilities of what had happened and how the man had died. Before he could get too close, an officer from the San Antonio Police Department stopped him.

"Hey, Doc. Good to see you again, sorry it has to be like this."

Calder didn't know the officer, but he wasn't surprised the man knew *him*. There weren't nearly as many MEs in the county as there were officers. "Yeah," he replied, wanting to get on with it. Dead bodies were a puzzle. A gruesome one, but a puzzle nonetheless. And he liked mysteries. Liked solving them. It was why he was such a good ME.

"I just wanted to let you know that if you need anything, I'll be over there interviewing the witnesses," the officer said.

Calder's head jerked up at that, and his attention strayed from the dead body for the first time. "Witnesses?"

"Yeah. I guess a woman and her kid were the ones who reported the DB. Called it in."

Having a witness could make his life easier, or it could make it more difficult. Many times, witness statements were incongruent with what the evidence was telling him. He didn't usually even read the statements until after he'd already examined the body and come to his own conclusions, but he always double checked what he believed happened, based on his examination, against the witness statements.

Although, the officer hadn't said the woman had witnessed anything, just that she'd notified the police of the location of the body.

"She doesn't look like she'll be much use though. I've found the waitresses at the diners downtown usually aren't all that bright."

Calder turned to look in the direction of where the cop indicated—and froze.

Standing off to the side, with a blanket around her shoulders, was a woman. And not just any woman. Hope Drayden. The person he'd been seeking for weeks.

The second he saw her, Calder knew it was Hope. Red hair, a backpack sitting on the ground at her feet, and a look of terror in her eyes. She was wearing a polyester uniform that he recognized from a chain of diners in and around San Antonio.

Standing next to her, with his head buried in her stomach, was a little boy. It had to be Billy. Calder knew it.

For the first time in his career, his focus wasn't on the body lying on the pavement in front of him. He needed to get to Hope and find out what the hell had happened. More importantly, he needed to get her and her son to Blythe. To safety.

He didn't know their story, but from the exhausted looks on both their faces, it was obvious they were at the end of their rope. He didn't know where they'd been living, but he was pleased that at least it seemed like Hope had a job, even though he had his doubts being a waitress would give her enough money to live off of long-term. He didn't think they'd been living on the streets recently, as he'd searched each and every shelter thoroughly and repeatedly over the last couple of weeks.

Without a word to the officer, Calder headed for the duo. He wasn't going to let them out of his sight. No way in hell. From this point on, he was going to be glued to their sides. It was obvious Hope needed a champion in the worst way, and she just got one.

* * *

Look for the next book in the series...*Justice for Hope.* *Find out where Hope and her son, Billy, have been and what Calder is going to do about their situation.*

JOIN my Newsletter and find out about sales, free books, contests and new releases before anyone else!! Click HERE

Want to know when my books go on sale? Follow me on Bookbub HERE!

Also by Susan Stoker

Badge of Honor: Texas Heroes Series

Justice for Mackenzie

Justice for Mickie

Justice for Corrie

Justice for Laine (novella)

Shelter for Elizabeth

Justice for Boone

Shelter for Adeline

Shelter for Sophie

Justice for Erin

Justice for Milena

Shelter for Blythe

Justice for Hope

Shelter for Quinn

Shelter for Koren

Shelter for Penelope

Delta Team Two Series

Shielding Gillian

Shielding Kinley (Aug 2020)

Shielding Aspen (Oct 2020)

Shielding Riley (Jan 2021)

Shielding Devyn (TBA)

Shielding Ember (TBA)

Shielding Sierra (TBA)

Delta Force Heroes Series

Rescuing Rayne

Rescuing Aimee (novella)

Rescuing Emily

Rescuing Harley

Marrying Emily (novella)

Rescuing Kassie

Rescuing Bryn

Rescuing Casey

Rescuing Sadie (novella)

Rescuing Wendy

Rescuing Mary

Rescuing Macie (novella)

SEAL of Protection: Legacy Series

Securing Caite

Securing Brenae (novella)

Securing Sidney

Securing Piper

Securing Zoey

Securing Avery (May 2020)

Securing Kalee (Sept 2020)

Ace Security Series

Claiming Grace

Claiming Alexis

Claiming Bailey

Claiming Felicity

Claiming Sarah

Mountain Mercenaries Series

Defending Allye

Defending Chloe

Defending Morgan

Defending Harlow

Defending Everly

Defending Zara

Defending Raven (June 2020)

Silverstone Series

Trusting Skylar (Dec 2020)

Trusting Taylor (TBA)

Trusting Molly (TBA)

Trusting Cassidy (TBA)

SEAL of Protection Series

Protecting Caroline

Protecting Alabama

Protecting Fiona

Marrying Caroline (novella)

Protecting Summer

Protecting Cheyenne

Protecting Jessyka
Protecting Julie (novella)
Protecting Melody
Protecting the Future
Protecting Kiera (novella)
Protecting Alabama's Kids (novella)
Protecting Dakota

Stand Alone

The Guardian Mist
Nature's Rift
A Princess for Cale
A Moment in Time- A Collection of Short Stories
Lambert's Lady

Special Operations Fan Fiction

http://www.AcesPress.com

Beyond Reality Series

Outback Hearts
Flaming Hearts
Frozen Hearts

Writing as Annie George:

Stepbrother Virgin (erotic novella)

ABOUT THE AUTHOR

New York Times, USA Today and *Wall Street Journal* Bestselling Author Susan Stoker has a heart as big as the state of Tennessee where she lives, but this all American girl has also spent the last twenty years living in Missouri, California, Colorado, Indiana, and Texas. She's married to a retired Army man who now gets to follow *her* around the country.

She debuted her first series in 2014 and quickly followed that up with the SEAL of Protection Series, which solidified her love of writing and creating stories readers can get lost in.

If you enjoyed this book, or any book, please consider leaving a review. It's appreciated by authors more than you'll know.

www.stokeraces.com
susan@stokeraces.com

facebook.com/authorsusanstoker

twitter.com/Susan_Stoker

instagram.com/authorsusanstoker

goodreads.com/SusanStoker

bookbub.com/authors/susan-stoker

amazon.com/author/susanstoker

Made in United States
Orlando, FL
26 May 2022

18217941R00178